TOKYO FIANCÉE

Amélie Nothomb

TOKYO FIANCÉE

*Translated from the French
by Alison Anderson*

Europa
editions

Europa Editions
116 East 16th Street
New York, N.Y. 10003
www.europaeditions.com
info@europaeditions.com

Translation by Alison Anderson
Original title: *Ni d'Eve ni d'Adam*

This work has been published thanks to support from
the French Ministry of Culture – Centre National du Livre
Ouvrage publié avec le concours du Ministère
Français chargé de la Culture – Centre National du Livre

Library of Congress Cataloging in Publication Data is available
ISBN 978-1-933372-64-8

Nothomb, Amélie
Tokyo Fiancée

Book design by Emanuele Ragnisco
www.mekkanografici.com

Cover photo © Catherine Cabrol

Printed in the United States of America

Prepress by Plan.ed – Rome

TOKYO FIANCÉE

The most efficient way to learn Japanese, it seemed, would be to teach French. I put an ad up at the supermarket: "French, private lessons, competitive rates." The phone rang that very evening. An appointment was made for the next day, at a café in Omote-Sando. I didn't understand his name at all, nor did he understand mine. As I was putting down the phone, I realized I had no idea how I would recognize him, nor would he know how to recognize me. And as I had not had the presence of mind to ask him for his number, that fact was unlikely to change. "Perhaps he'll call back to sort the matter out," I thought.

He didn't call back. His voice had seemed young. Not that that would help. There was no lack of young people in Tokyo in 1989. Particularly at a café in Omote-Sando, on January 26, at around three in the afternoon.

Nor was I the only foreign woman there, far from it. And yet he walked straight over to me.

"Are you the French teacher?"

"How did you know?"

He shrugged his shoulders. Very stiff, he sat down and said nothing. I understood that I was the teacher and it was up to me to attend to him. I asked some questions and learned that he was twenty years old, his name was Rinri, and he was studying French at university. He learned that I was twenty-one years old, my name was Amélie, and I was studying Japanese. He did not understand my nationality. I was used to that.

"From now on, we are not allowed to speak English," I said.

I conversed in French in order to determine his level; there was cause for consternation. The most serious problem was his pronunciation: if I had not known that Rinri was speaking to me in French, I would have thought I was dealing with a very weak beginning student in Chinese. His vocabulary was severely lacking, his syntax was a poor reproduction of English, which, for some absurd reason, seemed to be his frame of reference. And yet he was in his third year of French at university. This merely served to confirm the utter failure of language instruction in Japan: it was that bad, and it could no longer even be chalked up to insularity.

The young man must have been aware of the situation because before very long he apologized, then went quiet. I could not accept this defeat, so I tried to make him speak again. In vain. He kept his mouth shut as if to hide ugly teeth. We had reached an impasse.

So I began to speak to him in Japanese. I had not spoken it since I was five years old, and the six days I had just spent in the Land of the Rising Sun, after sixteen years away, had not sufficed to reactivate my childhood memories of the language—far from it. I came out with a flood of utterly meaningless, puerile gibberish involving a police officer, a dog, and some cherry blossoms.

The young man listened, stupefied, and eventually burst out laughing. He asked me if a five-year-old child had taught me to speak Japanese.

"Yes," I replied. "That child was me."

And I told him my story. I narrated it slowly, in French, and, thanks to a certain amount of emotion on my part, he seemed to actually understand me.

I had released him from his complexes.

In French that was worse than bad, he told me he knew the

region where I had been born and spent my first five years: Kansai.

He told me he was from Tokyo himself, where his father was director of a very important jewelry making school. Then he stopped, exhausted, and swallowed his coffee in one gulp.

His explanations seemed to have cost him an effort equal to that needed to ford a rushing river where the stepping stones are five yards apart. I watched with amusement as he caught his breath after such an exploit.

You have to admit that the French language is vicious. I would not have liked to be in my student's shoes. Learning to speak my language must be as difficult as learning to write his.

I asked him what he liked to do in life. He thought for a very long time. I wanted to find out whether his thoughts were of an existential or a linguistic nature. After his lengthy reflection, the reply he offered was very puzzling:

"Playing."

Impossible to determine whether the stumbling block was lexical or philosophical. I insisted, "Playing what?"

He shrugged his shoulders.

"Playing."

His attitude must have stemmed either from an admirable sense of detachment or from laziness in regard to learning my colossal language.

In either case, I decided that the boy had come out ahead, and I agreed with him wholeheartedly. I declared that he was quite right, that life was a game: those who believed that playing was no more than a futile activity simply didn't get it, etc.

He listened to me as if I were telling him the oddest things. The advantage of discussions with foreigners is that one can always, to varying degrees, attribute the other's consternation to cultural differences.

Rinri asked in turn what I liked in life. Carefully separating each syllable, I replied that I liked the sound of the rain, walking in the mountains, reading, writing, and listening to music. He interrupted me and said, "You like playing."

Why was he repeating his own idea? Perhaps to get my opinion on the topic. I continued, "Yes, I like to play, especially cards."

And now he was the one who seemed at a loss. On a blank page in a notebook I drew cards: ace, two, spades, diamonds.

He interrupted me: yes, of course, playing cards, he knew what I meant. I felt extraordinarily stupid with my worthless teaching methods. To land on my feet, I said the first thing that came into my head: what sort of food did he like to eat? Without a moment's hesitation he replied, "Omreeeh."

I thought I was familiar with Japanese cuisine, but this was something I had never heard of. I asked him to explain. Very soberly, he repeated, "Omreeeh."

Yes, naturally, but what was it?

Astonished, he took the notebook from my hands and drew the outline of an egg. It took me a few seconds to put the pieces of my brain back together and then I exclaimed, "Omelette!"

He opened his eyes as if to say, Obviously.

"It's pronounced oh-meh-let," I continued, "oh-meh-let."

"Omreeeh."

"No, look at my mouth. You need to open it wider: oh-meh-let."

He opened his mouth wide: "Omreeeht."

Was this progress, I wondered? Yes, because something had changed. There had been an evolution, if not exactly in the right direction, at least toward something else.

"That's better," I said, full of optimism.

He smiled without conviction, gratified by my politeness. I was the teacher he needed. He asked how much the lesson would cost.

"You may give me what you like."

This reply concealed my absolute ignorance of even the

approximate going rates. Without knowing it, I must have spoken like a true Japanese woman, for Rinri reached into his pocket and took out a lovely envelope in rice paper in which he had already slipped the money.

Embarrassed, I refused. "Not this time. This wasn't a lesson worthy of the name. It was just to get started."

The young man put the envelope down in front of me, went to pay for our coffees, and came back to make an appointment for the following Monday, ignored the envelope when I tried to return it to him, said goodbye, and took his leave.

Having swallowed all my shame, I opened the envelope and counted six thousand yen. The fabulous thing about being paid in a weak currency is that the amounts are always astronomical. I thought back on the "omreeeh" that had become an "omreee-ht," and felt I had not deserved six thousand yen.

I made a mental comparison between the wealth of Japan and the wealth of Belgium and concluded that this transaction was a mere drop of water in an ocean of considerable disproportion. With my six thousand yen I could buy six golden apples at the supermarket. Adam surely owed that much to Eve. My conscience at rest, I set off to wander around Omote-Sando.

J anuary 30, 1989. My tenth day in Japan as an adult. Every morning since the day of what I refer to as my return, I had opened the curtains onto a sky of perfect blue. For years I had opened Belgian curtains to find a sky leaden with gray—how could I fail to delight in the Tokyo winter?

I met my student at the café in Omote-Sando. The lesson focused on the weather. A good idea because the weather, an ideal topic for people who have nothing to say to each other, is the primary and obligatory topic of conversation in Japan.

To meet someone and fail to talk about the weather is to betray a lack of manners.

Rinri seemed to have made progress since our previous meeting. It could not be explained by my teaching alone: he must have been working on his own. No doubt the prospect of conversing with a Francophone had motivated him.

He was describing the rigors of summer when I saw him raise his eyes toward a boy who had just come in. They exchanged a sign.

"Who is that?" I asked.

"Hara, a friend who is a student with me."

The young man came over to greet us. Rinri made the introductions in English. I protested. "In French, please. Your friend is also studying the language."

My student began again, floundering somewhat because of the sudden change of register, then articulated as best he could, "Hara, I introduce Amélie, my mistress."

I was at great pains to hide my mirth, which would have discouraged such praiseworthy efforts. I would not correct him in front of his friend; that would have caused him to lose face.

It was a day of coincidences: into the café came Christine, a friendly young Belgian woman who worked at the embassy and had helped me with some paperwork.

I called her over.

I thought it must be my turn to make the introductions. But Rinri, now that he had gotten started, no doubt wished to repeat the exercise, and he said to Christine, "I introduce Hara, my friend, and Amélie, my mistress."

The young woman glanced at me. I simulated indifference and introduced Christine in turn to the young men. Because of the misunderstanding, and for fear of seeming a dominatrix in matters of love, I no longer dared give any instructions to my student. So I set as my only realistic goal that of maintaining French as the language of our exchange.

"You are both Belgium?" asked Hara.

"Yes," smiled Christine. "You both speak French very well."

"Thanks to Amélie who is my—"

At that moment I interrupted Rinri to say, "Hara and Rinri are studying French at university."

"Yes, but there's nothing like private lessons to really learn, is there?"

Christine's attitude was irritating, but I did not know her well enough to explain what was really going on.

"Where did you meet Amélie?" she asked Rinri.

"At the Azabu supermarket."

"How amusing!"

We had been spared the worst: he might have replied that it was through a personal ad.

The waitress came to take the order for the newcomers. Christine looked at her watch and said it was nearly time for her business appointment. As she was about to leave, she turned and spoke to me in Dutch.

"He's good-looking, I'm happy for you."

When she had left, Hara asked if she had been speaking Belgium. I nodded in order to avoid having to go into a long explanation.

"You speak French very well," said Rinri with admiration.

Yet another misunderstanding, I thought, overwhelmed.

I had run out of energy so, content with correcting their most incomprehensible errors, I asked Rinri and Hara to converse in French. What they said to each other astonished me.

"If you come to my house on Saturday, bring the Hiroshima sauce."

"Will Yasu play with us?"

"No, he is playing at Minami's."

I would have liked to know what they were playing. I put the question to Hara, whose reply was no more enlightening than the one my student had given me during the previous lesson.

"Saturday, you come too, come to play at my house," said Hara.

I am certain he was inviting me out of politeness. And yet I was very tempted to accept. I was worried that my presence might bother my student, so I tested the waters, "I don't know Tokyo, I'll get lost."

"I will come and get you," offered Rinri.

Reassured, I thanked Hara enthusiastically. When Rinri handed me the envelope containing my fee, I was even more embarrassed than the previous time. I soothed my conscience by deciding to earmark the money for a gift for my host.

On Saturday afternoon I saw a magnificent white Mercedes pull up outside my lodging, so clean that it sparkled in the sun. As I walked toward it the door opened automatically. Behind the wheel was my student.

As we drove through Tokyo, I wondered if his father's profession was not a front for membership in the Yakuza, Mercedes being their vehicle of choice. But I kept my musings to myself. Rinri drove without speaking, concentrating on the heavy traffic.

I glanced over at his profile, remembering what Christine had said to me in Dutch. I would never have thought to find him handsome if my compatriot had not pointed it out to me. Moreover, I was not convinced that he was handsome. But the stiffness of his closely shaven nape and the absolute immobility of his features were not without an impressive distinction.

This was the third time I had seen him. He always wore the same clothes: jeans, a white T-shirt, and a black suede jacket. On his feet he wore what looked like cosmonaut's boots. His slim build fascinated me.

A car cut in front of him in the rudest way. Not satisfied with a mere violation, the driver got out and hurled insults at Rinri. My student remained very calm, proffering humble apologies. The lout stormed off.

"But he was in the wrong!" I protested.

"Yes," said Rinri phlegmatically.

"Why did you apologize?"

"I don't know the word in French."

"Say it in Japanese."

"*Kankokujin.*"

Korean. I understood. I smiled to myself at my student's polite fatalism.

Hara lived in a microscopic apartment. His friend handed him an enormous carton of Hiroshima sauce. I felt like an idiot with my six-pack of Belgian beer, although it was greeted with sincere curiosity.

Among the guests was a certain Masa, who was slicing cabbage into fine shreds, and a young American woman called Amy. Her presence obliged us to speak English, which made her hateful to me. I disliked her even more when I realized that she had been invited in the hope of making me feel more at ease. As if I would suffer from being the only Westerner.

Amy seemed to think that this was a good time to tell us how she was suffering in exile. What did she miss the most? Peanut butter, she said, deadly serious. Every one of her sentences began with, "In Portland . . ." The three boys listened politely although it was fairly obvious that they did not know which coast was home to her hick town, nor did they care. As for me, though I despised simplistic anti-Americanism, I thought that to forbid myself from hating this girl because she was American would in fact constitute an unspeakable form of simplistic anti-Americanism: I indulged, therefore, in pure and simple loathing.

Rinri was peeling ginger, Hara was preparing shrimp, and Masa had finished shredding the cabbage. In my mind I added the Hiroshima sauce and exclaimed, interrupting Amy in the middle of a sentence about Portland, "We're having *okonomiyaki!*"

"You know it?" asked my host, surprised.

"It was my favorite dish when I lived in Kansai!"

"You lived in Kansai?" asked Hara.

Rinri had not told him a thing about me. Had he even understood a word of what I had said during the first lesson? Suddenly I blessed Amy's presence for obliging us to speak English, and I explained my Japanese past with a tremor in my voice.

"Do you have Japanese nationality?" interrupted Masa.

"No. It's not enough to be born here. There isn't a single nationality as difficult to obtain as Japanese."

"You can become American," suggested Amy.

To avoid making a gaffe I quickly changed the subject. "I'd like to give a hand. Where are the eggs?"

"Please, you are my guest," said Hara. "Sit down and play."

I looked all around me for a game, but in vain. Amy saw my confusion and burst out laughing.

"*Asobu*," she said.

"Yes, *asobu*, to play, I know," I replied.

"No, you don't know. The verb *asobu* doesn't mean the same thing as the verb *to play*. In Japanese, the minute you're not working, it's *asobu*."

So that was it. I was furious that it was a native of Portland who had taught me this and I immediately launched into a pedantic retort in order to put her in her place.

"I see. So it corresponds to the notion of *otium* in Latin."

"Latin?" answered Amy, terrified.

Delighted by her reaction, I compared *otium* with Ancient Greek, and no Indo-European etymology was spared. She was about to find out what a philologist was, Miss Native of Portland.

Now that I had forced her to surrender her ill-gotten gains, I fell silent and began to play in the Rising Sun manner. I watched contemplatively as the pancake batter was prepared, then as the *okonomiyaki* were cooked. The aroma of cabbage, shrimp and ginger sizzling together carried me sixteen years into the past, to the era when my gentle governess Nishio-san would concoct the same magnificent treat for me, and which I have not tasted since.

Hara's apartment was so small that I could not overlook a single detail. Rinri opened the box of Hiroshima sauce along the dotted line and set it down in the middle of the low table. "What's that?" whined Amy. I grabbed the carton and inhaled the nostalgic fragrance of bitter plum, vinegar, saké and soy. As if I were getting high on Tetra Pak.

When I was given my plate of stuffed pancake, I lost my veneer of civilization, poured sauce over the dish and dug in.

There are no Japanese restaurants anywhere in the world outside Japan that serve this popular dish, so terribly evocative, both simple and subtle, down-to-earth and sophisticated. I was five years old again, I had never been out of sight of my Nishio-san, and I was screaming, broken-hearted, my taste buds in a trance. I devoured my *okonomiyaki* and my eyes glazed over as I uttered faint little cries of delight.

Only when I had eaten everything on my plate did I notice that the others were staring politely, embarrassed.

"Every country has its own table manners," I muttered. "You've just discovered the Belgians'."

"Oh my God!" shrieked Amy.

She was a fine one to talk. No matter what she had in her mouth, she looked as if she were chewing gum.

My host's reaction was far more gratifying: he rushed to prepare another pancake for me.

We were drinking Kirin beer. I had brought some Chimay, which would have tasted somewhat bizarre alongside the Hiroshima sauce. Asian barley beers, on the other hand, go well with meals.

I have no clue what the guests talked about. I was too overwhelmed by what I was eating, in the midst of a journey into memory of such poignant intensity that I could not hope to share it.

I recall through a sort of emotional fog that Amy went on to suggest a game of Pictionary, and so we played in the Western sense of the word. She very quickly regretted her suggestion: the Japanese are far too clever when it comes to drawing a concept. The game was played by the three Japanese, while I digested in ecstasy and the American girl lost, shouting angrily. She was infinitely grateful for my presence, because I played even more badly than she did. Whenever it was my turn I traced something on the paper that vaguely resembled French fries.

"Come on!" she grumbled, while the three boys gradually abandoned any effort to hide their mirth.

It was an excellent evening, and when it was over Rinri drove me home.

A t the next lesson, I noticed his behavior had changed: he addressed me more like a friend than like a teacher. This pleased me, and all the more so as it seemed to encourage his progress: he was less shy about speaking. Conversely, I found it far more awkward to accept the envelope.

When it was time to leave, Rinri asked me why I always arranged our meetings at a café in Omote-Sando.

"I've hardly been in Tokyo for more than two weeks, so I don't know any other cafés. If you know of any good places, please don't hesitate to suggest one."

He replied that he would come and get me with the car.

In the meantime, my course in business Japanese had started, and I found myself in a classroom with Singaporeans, Germans, Canadians, and Koreans, who all believed that learning Japanese was the key to success. There was even an Italian, but before very long he threw in the towel, unable to resist the temptation to stress syllables.

The pronunciation errors of the Germans, who insisted on saying *v* instead of *w,* seemed minor in comparison. As always in my life, I was the only Belgian.

On the weekend I was able to travel outside Tokyo for the first time. I went by train to the little town of Kamakura, an hour from the capital. The rediscovery of this ancient, silent Japan brought tears to my eyes. Beneath a sky of intense blue, the roofs heavy with cascading tiles and the air motionless with frost told me that they had been waiting for me, that they had missed me, that the order of the world had been restored by my return and that my reign would last ten thousand years.

There has always been a megalomaniacal bent to my lyricism.

On Monday afternoon, the too-white Mercedes opened its door to me.

"Where are we going?"

"To my house," said Rinri.

I did not know what to say. His house? He was insane. He ought to have told me beforehand. What strange manners on the part of such a well-brought-up Japanese boy!

Perhaps my premonition about his belonging to the Yakuza was justified. I looked closely at his wrists: were any tattoos discernible beyond the sleeves of his jacket? And his perfectly shaven neck: what allegiance might that signify?

After a long ride we arrived in the luxurious neighborhood of Den-en-chofu, where the wealthy of Tokyo are housed. A garage door lifted before us upon recognizing the car. The house represented what the 1960s in Japan must have considered to be the height of modernity. A garden six feet wide surrounded the house, a sort of green moat for this square concrete château.

His parents greeted me by calling me Sensei, which gave me a terrible urge to laugh. Rinri's father looked like a contemporary work of art, exquisite and incomprehensible, covered in platinum jewelry. His mother, far more ordinary, was wearing an elegant, respectable suit. I was served some green tea, then very quickly we were left alone, so that the quality of my teaching would not be adversely affected.

How could I rise to the occasion? I could not imagine myself making him repeat "omelette" in this intergalactic space station. Why had I been brought here? Did he have any idea of the effect it was having on me? Apparently not.

"Have you always lived in this house?" I asked.

"Yes."

"It's magnificent."

"No."

He did not have the right to reply in any other way. Yet it was not completely untrue. In spite of everything, the house retained a certain simplicity. In any other country, a family as rich as this one would have lived in a palace. But when compared with the standard of living in Tokyo—to his friend Hara's apartment, for example—a villa like this left one feeling dazed by its size, its presence, and its tranquility.

I continued the lesson as best I could, struggling to avoid any talk of the mansion or of his parents. And yet a feeling of malaise would not leave me. I had the distinct impression that I was being watched. This could only be the result of paranoia: Rinri's parents had far too much class to stoop to such a pastime.

Gradually I began to sense that Rinri shared my suspicions. He was looking around warily. Was the concrete château haunted by a ghost? He interrupted me with a gesture and set off on tiptoes toward the stairwell.

He let out a shout and suddenly, like two jack-in-the-boxes, there appeared a little old man and a little old lady who shrieked with laughter and manifold hilarity upon seeing me.

"Sensei, I would like to introduce my grandmother and grandfather."

"Sensei! Sensei!" squealed the old people, who seemed to think that I looked about as much like a professor as a slide trombone.

"How do you do."

The least little thing I said, the least little gesture, set them off giggling like lunatics. They made faces, slapped their grandson on the back, then slapped me on the back; they drank the tea from my cup. The old woman touched my forehead and shouted, "How white it is!" then fell over laughing, followed by her husband.

Rinri smiled as he looked at them, never losing his composure. It occurred to me that they must actually be senile, and that Rinri's parents were perfectly admirable to be sheltering such crackpot old dodderers in their home. After an interlude of ten minutes or so, my student bowed to his ancestors and begged them to kindly return to their chambers to get some rest, for they must be tired after such exertion.

The horrible old people eventually complied, once they had roundly taken the mickey out of me.

I did not understand everything they said, but the message was clear enough. Once they had disappeared, I looked questioningly at the young man. But he said nothing.

"Your grandparents are . . . special," I commented.

"They are old," replied the boy, soberly.

"Did anything happen to them?" I insisted.

"They got old."

This could go round in circles. Changing the subject was a tour de force. I noticed a Bang & Olufsen stereo and asked what sort of music he listened to. He talked about Ryuichi Sakamoto. One thing led to another and we made it to the end of a lesson that had been exceptionally trying. When I received the envelope, I reflected that I had worked hard for it. He drove me home without saying a word.

I asked around, and learned that this is a common phenomenon in Japan. In a land where people must behave well all their lives, what often happens is that on the verge of old age they snap, and allow themselves the most outlandish behavior, and yet their families still look after them, in keeping with tradition.

This seemed absolutely heroic. But at night I was assailed by nightmares, where Rinri's ancestors pulled my hair and pinched my cheeks, croaking with laughter.

When the immaculate Mercedes again offered me its hospitality, I hesitated to climb in.

"Are we going to your home?"

"Yes."

"You aren't afraid we'll disturb your parents and, above all, your grandparents?"

"No, they've gone on a trip."

I climbed in next to him.

He drove without speaking. I loved the way we could dispense with chatter to such a degree and never feel the least bit ill at ease. It gave me the opportunity to get a better look at the city and, in passing, at my student's incredibly motionless profile.

At his house he made green tea for me, but opened a Coke for himself—a detail which amused me because he did not even ask me my opinion. It went without saying that a foreigner could enjoy such Japanese refinement, whereas he had already had his fill of all things Japanese.

"Where did your family go?"

"To Nagoya. That's where my grandparents are from."

"Do you ever go there?"

"No, it's a boring place."

I liked his straightforward replies. I found out that they were his mother's parents. His paternal grandparents had passed away, something I learned not without relief: consequently, there could not be more than two monsters in the realm.

Out of curiosity I asked him to show me around the house. He did not take offense, and guided me through a labyrinth of rooms and stairways. The kitchen and bathroom were worth their weight in computer gadgetry. The bedrooms were fairly simple, especially Rinri's: a basic bed with a bookshelf along the side. I looked at the titles: the complete works of Kaiko Takeshi, his favorite author, as well as Stendhal and Sartre. I knew that the Japanese worshipped Sartre, found him terribly exotic: to feel nauseous upon contemplating a pebble polished by the sea was so contrary to prevailing Japanese attitudes, and something so very strange could not fail to fascinate.

Stendhal's presence pleased me immensely and was a greater surprise. I told Rinri that Stendhal was one of my gods. He melted. I saw him smile as never before.

"It's delightful," he said.

He was right.

"You are a good reader."

"I think I've spent my life on this bed, reading."

I looked with emotion at my student's futon, imagining the years he had spent there with a book in his hand.

"You've made a great deal of progress in French," I observed.

He pointed at me with his open hand by way of explanation.

"No, I'm not that much of a teacher . . . It's thanks to your own efforts."

He shrugged his shoulders.

On the way home, outside a museum he noticed a poster that to me was illegible.

"Would you like to visit this exhibition?" he asked.

Did I feel like visiting an exhibition I knew absolutely nothing about? Yes.

"I'll come and get you tomorrow afternoon," he said.

I liked the idea that I did not know whether I would be seeing paintings, sculpture or a retrospective of various thingam-ajigs. One should always go to exhibitions in this way, on the off chance, without knowing a thing about them. Someone wants to show us something: that is all that matters.

The following evening, I had no better understanding of the theme of the exhibition. There were a number of paintings that were probably modern, but I couldn't be certain: and bas-reliefs about which I was incapable of saying a single word. Very quickly I realized that it was in the rooms of the museum itself that there was something to see. It was the Tokyo public that fascinated me most: the way they would stop respectfully in front of each work and observe it for a long time with the utmost gravity.

Rinri did the same. Eventually I asked him, "Do you like it?"

"I don't know."

"Does it interest you?"

"Not much."

I burst out laughing. People looked at me uncomfortably.

"What would it be if it were interesting to you?"

He didn't understand my question; I didn't insist.

On the way out of the museum someone was handing out fliers. I could not decipher them but I loved the zeal with which everyone accepted their flier and read it. Rinri must have for-gotten that I scarcely had any mastery of ideograms because once he had read his flier he asked me, pointing to the paper, whether I would like to go there. Nothing could be more irre-sistible than the words "go there" when "there" is unknown. I accepted enthusiastically.

"I'll come and get you the day after tomorrow in the evening," he said.

I exulted in the fact that I did not know whether we were going to an anti-nuclear demonstration, some video-artist's happening, or a Butoh performance. It was impossible to pre-dict the dress code, so I dressed in a more neutral fashion than ever. I wagered that Rinri would be wearing his usual outfit. He was indeed disguised as himself when he took me to what turned out to be a gallery opening.

The artist was Japanese and I have taken great pains to forget his name. His paintings seemed so boring they defied any competition, but this did not prevent the Japanese visitors from showing each work the admirable respect and sublime patience for which they are renowned. An evening like this would have reconciled me with humankind had the artist himself not been so painfully present. I was at pains to believe that this man who must have been in his mid-fifties belonged to the same species, so very odious was he. A number of people went up to congratulate him or even buy one or two of his canvases, which were horribly expensive. He would eye the buyers scornfully, no doubt considering them some sort of necessary evil. I could not help but go up to speak to him.

"Excuse me, but I cannot seem to understand your art. Could you explain it to me?"

"There is nothing to understand, nothing to explain," he replied with disgust. "It is meant to be felt."

"Precisely—I don't feel anything."

"That's your loss."

I needn't be told twice. Upon reflection, it seemed to me that there was a certain integrity in his words. The lesson I learned at this opening was one I have never needed, of course: that is, if I were to become an artist one day, regardless of whether I had any talent or not, I would exhibit my work in Japan. The Japanese public are the best in the world and, what's more, they buy. Irrespective of the sums involved, how lovely it must be for artists to see their work become the object of so much thoughtful consideration!

At the following lesson, Rinri asked me to explain the use of the formal pronoun *vous*. I was astonished that this issue was still problematic for a speaker of a language which already involved such a complicated mastery of politeness.

"Yes," he said. "But you and I say *vous* to each other. Why?"

"Because I am your teacher."

He accepted my explanation without protesting. I thought for a moment and added, "If it is a problem for you, we could decide to say *tu* instead."

"No, no," he said, careful to respect something he seemed to consider established usage.

I steered the lesson toward more ordinary considerations. At the end, as he was handing me the envelope, Rinri asked if he could come and collect me on Saturday afternoon.

"To go where?" I asked.

"To play."

I adored this answer, so I accepted.

I too was taking classes, making progress in Japanese as best I could. It hadn't taken me long to earn a bad reputation. Whenever I was intrigued by a certain detail, I would raise my hand. My various teachers nearly had a heart attack every time they saw me brandishing my fingers skyward. I thought they had gone silent to allow me to speak and I boldly asked my question, but the answer I was given was curiously unsatisfying.

This went on until one day one of my teachers, on seeing that I had performed my customary gesture yet again, began to shout with formidable violence.

"Enough!"

I was stunned, while all the students stared at me intently.

After class I went to apologize to the teacher, above all to determine the nature of my crime.

"One must not ask questions of the Sensei," scolded the teacher.

"But—if I do not understand?"

"You understand!"

I now knew why language instruction in Japan was so wobbly.

There was also the episode where each of the students had to give a presentation on his or her native country. When my turn came, I had the distinct impression that I had been awarded a particularly difficult case. The others had been talking about well-known countries. I was the only one who had to specify the continent in which my nation was located. I came to regret the presence of the German students, for if they hadn't been there I could have made up anything I liked, pointing on the map to an island in the middle of the South Seas, evoking odd customs such as asking questions of the professor. But I had to stick to a classical exposé, observing all the while that the students from Singapore were applying toothpicks to their gold teeth with a vigor that distressed me greatly.

On Saturday afternoon the Mercedes seemed whiter than ever.

I was told that we were going to Hakone. As I knew nothing about the place, I asked for additional information. Rinri hemmed and hawed a bit then said that I would see. The road seemed endless: a never-ending series of toll booths.

We eventually arrived at a vast lake surrounded by hills and picturesque *torii* gates. People come here to take small boat trips or hire pedal boats. The idea of pedal boats made me want to laugh. Hakone was the preferred Sunday outing of Tokyo dwellers with a Romantic bent.

We plied the waves on a sort of ferry. I delighted in the spectacle of Japanese families admiring their surroundings as they vigorously wiped their little one's behind, or of lovers in their lovers' garments, hand in hand.

"Have you already brought your lady love to this place?" I asked.

"I have no lady love."

"Have you ever had a lady love?"

"Yes. I did not bring her here."

I was thus the first lady to have the honor. It must have been because I was a foreigner.

On the boat a loudspeaker was broadcasting sappy songs. We docked by a *torii,* disembarked and set off along a well-marked poetic path. Couples stopped in spots specifically conceived for the purpose and gazed with emotion at the view of the lake through the *torii.* Children whined, as if to warn all lovers of the future that awaited them after so much romanticism. I was having a good time.

After our nautical jaunt, Rinri offered me a *kori:* I adored this shaved ice cream drizzled with green-tea syrup. I had not tasted it since childhood. Such a lovely crisp sensation when you bite into it.

On the way back, I wondered why this young man had brought me to Hakone. Naturally I was enchanted by what was a typical Japanese excursion, but why exactly had he wanted to share it with me? No doubt I was asking myself too many questions. More than in any other country on earth, the Japanese did things because they were done. And that was all well and good.

I began to sense that Rinri was expecting an invitation to my place. It would have been the polite thing to do: after all, I had been to his home so many times.

And yet I obstinately refused to entertain the idea. Inviting anyone to my house has always been a terrible ordeal. By definition, for reasons that I am at pains to explain, *chez moi* is no place for a decent person to visit.

From the day I obtained my independence, all premises inhabited by my own self have immediately come to resemble a junk-room for political refugees to squat in, ready to make a quick getaway at the slightest hint of a police raid.

At the beginning of March, I had a phone call from Christine. She was going to Belgium for a month to see her mother, and she asked me to house-sit for her and water the plants. I agreed and went by her place. I could not believe my eyes: she was a resident of the nec plus ultra of avant-garde Tokyo accommodation: a sublime apartment in a futuristic building, with a view of other futuristic buildings. My mouth agape, I listened as Christine explained the operating instructions for her modern marvel: everything was computerized. The plants seemed like some vestige of prehistory whose sole purpose was to serve as a pretext for the likes of me to live in such a palace for a month.

I impatiently awaited Christine's departure and then took up residence at her interplanetary station. Beyond a doubt: I was no longer *chez moi*. In every room there was a remote control to program not only the music, but also the temperature and anything else that might be going on in the other rooms. I could lie in bed and cook dinner in the microwave, turn on the washing machine, or lower the blinds in the living room.

Moreover, the building was located a stone's throw from the Ichigaya barracks where Mishima had committed his ritual suicide. I felt as if I was living in a place of extraordinary significance, and I could not stop pacing up and down the apartment, listening to Bach, observing the mistery of how well the harpsichord complemented this phantasm of an urban panorama, with its too-blue sky.

In the kitchen the intelligent toaster expelled its slices the moment they were perfectly cooked. At that point you would hear a delightful little chime. In fact, I was able to program entire concerts by means of the beeps from the household appliances.

I had given the telephone number of Christine's place to only one person, and he did not take long to call.

"How is the apartment?" asked Rinri.

"It would seem quite normal to you. To me it is incredible. Come over on Monday for the lesson and you'll see."

"Monday? Today's Friday. That's a long time. Could I come over this evening?"

"For dinner? I can't cook."

"I'll take care of everything."

I did not manage to come up with a pretext for refusing, particularly as I really did like the idea. This was the first time that my student had shown himself to be enterprising. No doubt Christine's apartment had something to do with it. Neutral territory changes the whole setup.

At seven that evening I saw the boy's face on the screen of the intercom, and I opened the door. He was carrying a brand new suitcase.

"Are you going on a trip?"

"No, I'm coming to cook at your place."

I took him on a tour of the domain, which seemed less enchanted to him than it had to me.

"It's fine," he said. "Do you like Swiss-cheese fondue?"

"Yes. Why?"

"So much the better. I brought the equipment."

Over time I would discover the veritable worship which the Japanese devote to all the various equipment one might conceivably ever use in life: equipment for mountains, equipment for the sea, equipment for golf and, this evening, equipment for Swiss-cheese fondue. At Rinri's house there was a neat, orderly room with suitcases at the ready if one were called on to perform a specific function.

Thus, before my enthralled gaze the young man opened this specific suitcase and in it I beheld, each item securely fixed in its own spot, an intergalactic-propulsion spirit burner, a nonstick fondue pot, a pouch of cheese in expanded polystyrene, a bottle of antifreeze white wine and slices of imputrescible bread. He transferred these remarkable items onto the Plexiglas table.

"Shall I begin?" he inquired.

"Yes, I'm eager to see what you're going to do."

He poured the polystyrene and the antifreeze into the fondue pot, lit the burner which, oddly enough, failed to lift off toward the stratosphere and, while these substances were fomenting various chemical reactions, he unpacked two pseudo-Tyrolian plates, two long forks and two stem glasses, "for the rest of the wine."

I ran to fetch some Coke from the fridge, assuring him that it would go very nicely with cheese fondue, and I filled my stem glass.

"It's ready," he announced.

We sat bravely across from one another and I ventured to

place a small piece of imputrescible bread onto the edge of the fork, and then dipped it into the mixture. I removed it and marveled at the fantastic number of strings which immediately formed.

"Yes," said Rinri proudly, "the strings have turned out most satisfactorily."

The strings, as we all know, are the true purpose of cheese fondue. I placed the object in my mouth and began to chew: it had absolutely no taste. I understood that the Japanese love to eat cheese fondue for the playful aspect of the thing, and that they had managed to create a version that eliminated the only unfortunate aspect of this traditional dish: its taste.

"It's delicious," I agreed, hiding my mirth.

Rinri felt hot and I was seeing him for the first time without his black suede jacket. I went to fetch a bottle of Tabasco, assuring him that in Belgium we ate cheese fondue with red-pepper sauce. I dipped a piece of bread into the hot poly-styrene (eliciting a web of a thousand strings), placed the yellow cube onto my plate, and splashed it with Tabasco so that it would have some taste. The boy watched my little game and I swear I could read the following conclusion in his eyes: "Belgians are very odd." He was a fine one to talk.

I soon wearied of my modern-style fondue.

"Go on, Rinri, tell me something."

"But . . . you just said *tu* to me!"

"When you've shared a fondue like this one with somebody, you have to say *tu,* no more standing on ceremony."

The polystyrene must have still been expanding in my brain, which was synthetizing the growth in the form of a delirium of experimentation. While Rinri was racking his brains to try to come up with something to tell me, I blew out the flame on the burner, something that surprised my Japanese friend, then proceeded to empty the rest of the antifreeze into the mixture to cool it down; and I plunged both hands into the sticky mass.

My host let out a cry. "Why did you do that?"

"Just to see."

I removed my paws and played with the skein of strings that now connected them. A thick layer of fake cheese had given me gloves.

"How are you going to wash it off?"

"With soap and water."

"No, it's too sticky. The pot is non-stick but not your hands."

"We'll soon find out."

And indeed, the stream of water from the tap and the dish washing detergent made no headway against my yellow mittens.

"I'll try to peel my hands with a kitchen knife."

Before Rinri's terrified gaze I set my plan in motion. What was bound to happen did happen: I cut a gash in my palm, and blood spurted through the plasticized membrane. I raised my wound to my lips to keep from turning the place into a crime scene.

"May I?" asked the boy.

He went down on his knees and took one of my hands and began to scrape it with his teeth. This was undoubtedly the best method, but the spectacle of this knight genuflecting before his lady and holding her fingers so delicately in order to gnaw at polystyrene caused me to burst out laughing. Never in my life had I been so confounded by gallantry.

Rinri remained quite unruffled and scraped away to the end. The operation lasted countless minutes during which I became increasingly aware of the oddity of the situation. And then, consummate craftsman that he was, he cleaned my fingers in the sink with detergent and an abrasive sponge.

When the work was done, he scrutinized his rescue operation and sighed with relief. The episode had been a catharsis for him. He took me in his arms and kept me there.

The next morning I was awoken by the sensation of painfully dry hands. As I was rubbing them with cream, I recalled the previous evening, and the night. So there was a boy in my bed. How should I proceed?

I went to rouse him from his sleep and told him very gently that, in my country, tradition required that the man depart at dawn. We had already broken with that tradition, for the sun had risen. We would put our dereliction of duty down to geographical distance. However, we must not take undue advantage of this excuse. Rinri asked me if Belgian tradition would allow us to meet again.

"Yes," I replied.

"I'll come and get you at three this afternoon."

I noted with pleasure that my lessons on the use of the informal pronoun had borne their fruit. Upon parting he was very sweet. I watched him leave with his Swiss-cheese fondue suitcase.

As soon as I was alone I felt a great rush of joy. I contemplated the events with a mixture of mirth and astonishment. What stunned me the most, when all is said and done, was not Rinri's own peculiar foibles, but rather this supreme eccentricity: here was someone who was likeable and charming. He had never treated me unkindly in word or deed. I had not known that this existed.

I made my half-liter of too-strong tea and sipped it while I looked out at the Ichigaya barracks. I had no desire to commit seppuku this morning. Rather, I felt a phenomenal need to write. Let Tokyo take shelter from the shock wave: we would see what we would see. I threw myself at the blank page convinced that the earth would move.

Oddly enough, there was no earthquake. Given the area where we lived, such telluric tranquility was an oddity that might be attributable to certain auspicious circumstances.

At times I would pause in my writing and look out at Tokyo through the bay window and think: "I'm having an affair with a man from this place." I would be dumbfounded, then return to my writing. The entire day went by in this manner. Such days are altogether excellent.

The next morning, the punctuality of the Mercedes was equaled only by its white sheen.

Rinri had changed. His profile as a driver was no longer as immobile and impassive. His silence deepened, with an interesting awkwardness.

"Where are we going?" I asked.

"You'll see."

This reply would become classic Rinri: whether our destination was grandiose or merely trivial, my questions would never elicit anything other than "you'll see." Youlsee was this boy's Cytherea: a changeable place whose sole purpose was to provide direction for the car.

That Sunday inaugurated the Youlsee of the Tokyo variety: the Olympic park. The idea seemed a good one, insofar as it had a certain significance, but I was indifferent to it: even beneath the most noble banners, competitions have never managed to arouse my interest. I observed the stadium and sporting facilities with the ideal polite gaze of lukewarm interest, I listened to Rinri's parsimonious explanations, and I focused my attention solely on his progress in French: in the Olympic games for foreign language learning, he would get the gold.

We were far from being the only lovers—to use the customary designation—who were walking around the stadium. I adored this "required visit" side of our tribulations: tradition, in Japan, meant that couples for a day or for a lifetime had at their disposal an entire infrastructure guaranteed to forestall any insecurity about how to spend one's time together. It was like a parlor game. You have feelings for someone? Instead of complicating the issue by trying to determine what, exactly, is affecting you, take that person with you to such-and-such square on the monopoly board, or rather monophyly board. Why monophyly? You'll see.

Youlsee was the best philosophy. Rinri and I had no idea what we were doing together or where we were headed. While pretending to be visiting places that were only relatively interesting, we were exploring each other with a kindly curiosity. Square one of Japanese monophyly, so far, was proving enchanting.

Rinri took me by the hand, just as all the lovers on the required visit held the hand of the lady they were with. As we stood by the podium he said to me, "This is the podium."

"Ah," I replied.

At the pool he said, "This is the pool."

"So it is," I answered, serious as can be.

I would not have changed places with anyone. I was having too much fun, and I encouraged further revelations, such as, when we were walking toward the boxing ring, "This is the boxing ring," and so on. Rinri's running commentary filled me with delight.

At five in the afternoon, like many of the local lovers, I was offered a pomegranate *kori*. I bit enthusiastically into the colored crushed ice. I noticed that this inspired tender displays of gratitude in the generous donors around me, and I did not stint on my performance. I enjoyed the idea that I was copying the reactions of the women around me.

As night fell it grew cold. I asked Rinri what the monophyly had in store for the evening.

"Pardon?" he asked.

To help him out of an awkward position, I invited him to Christine's place. He seemed equally delighted and relieved.

Youlsee was at its most fantastic within the four walls of the avant-garde Tokyo apartment building. Strains of Bach greeted us the moment I opened the door.

"This is Bach," I said.

To each his own.

"I like it very much," said Rinri.

I turned and pointed straight at him.

"It's you."

After love, there were no rules. On the pillow I discovered someone. He looked at me for a very long time and then said, "How handsome you are."

I wouldn't have corrected him for the world. No one has ever called me handsome.

"Japanese women are far more handsome," I said.

"That's not true."

I delighted in his bad taste.

"Tell me about Japanese girls."

He shrugged. I insisted. He finally said, "I can't explain. They annoy me. They aren't themselves."

"Maybe I'm not myself either."

"Yes you are. You are there, you exist, you look around. But they are always wondering if you like them. They only think about themselves."

"Most Western girls are exactly the same."

"My friends and I get the impression that, for those girls, we are mirrors."

I pretended to look at myself in his face, fixing my hair. He laughed.

"Do you talk a lot about girls with your friends?"

"Not a lot. It's awkward. And you, do you talk about boys?"

"No, it's private."

"With Japanese girls it's the opposite. They're very modest around the boy, then they go and tell everything to their girl-friends."

"Western girls do the same."

"Why do you say that?"

"To defend the Japanese girls. It must be hard to be a Japanese woman."

"It's also hard to be a Japanese man."

"I'm sure it is. Tell me."

He went quiet. He took a breath. I saw his features become transformed.

"When I was five, like all the other children, I took the tests to enter one of the best primary schools. If I passed, it meant that one day I could go to one of the best universities. I knew this at the age of five. But I didn't pass."

I noticed that he was trembling.

"My parents said nothing. They were disappointed. My father, at the age of five, had passed the tests. I waited until it was nighttime and then I cried."

He burst into tears. I gathered him into my arms. He was tense with suffering. I had heard of this terrible selection process in Japan, imposed a thousand years too early on children who were all too aware of what was at stake.

"At the age of five I found out I was not intelligent enough."

"That's not true. At the age of five you found out you had not been selected."

"I thought my father must be thinking, 'It's nothing serious. He's my son, he'll take my place.' My shame began there and has never gone away."

I held him close, murmuring words of comfort, assuring him of his intelligence. He cried for a long time, then fell asleep.

I went to look out at the night, at a city where every year the majority of five-year-old children learn that they have missed their chance in life. I thought I could hear the echoes of a symphony of stifled tears.

Rinri would make it because he was his father's son: he would replace his pain with shame. But other children who had failed the tests knew from a very young age that they would, at best, become corporate fodder, just as there used to be cannon fodder. It is no wonder that so many young Japanese commit suicide.

Christine would not be coming back for another three weeks. I suggested to Rinri that we should take full advantage of her apartment. The monophyly game could be continued after her return. The young man was delighted with my suggestion.

In love, as in anything, infrastructure is everything. I looked out the bay window onto the Ichigaya barracks and asked Rinri if he liked Mishima.

"Magnificent," he said.

"You surprise me. I have been told that as a writer he's more popular with Europeans."

"The Japanese don't like his personality. But his work is sublime. It's strange your European friends have said that to you, because it's above all in Japanese that his writing is beautiful. His sentences are music. How can you translate that?"

I was thrilled by what Rinri had said. As it would be a long time before I could decipher the necessary ideograms, I asked him to read some Mishima out loud to me, in the original. He graciously complied and, as I listened to him reading *Kinjiki,* I felt a shiver. But by no means could I understand everything—the title to begin with.

"Why *Forbidden Colors?*"

"In Japanese, color can be synonymous with love."

For a long time homosexuality in Japan was forbidden by law. However delightful the equivalence between color and love might be, Rinri was touching on a delicate subject. I never spoke of love; he often brought it up; I managed to change the subject. We were looking out the window through the binoculars: Japan's cherry trees were in bloom.

"Tradition says that I should sing to you while we drink saké under the cherry trees in the night."

"You're on."

Under the nearest cherry tree, Rinri sang witty little ditties to me. I laughed, he sulked.

"I believe what I am singing."

I swallowed the saké in one go to rid myself of my awkwardness. These budding blossoms were dangerous, exalting the young man's sentimentalism in this way.

Back in the technological apartment, I felt safe once again. Error: I was treated to words of love as high and wide as the building. I listened bravely and said nothing. Fortunately, the young man accepted my silence.

I liked him a great deal. But you cannot say that to someone who is in love with you. A pity. For me, liking him a great deal was already a . . . great deal.

He made me happy.

I was always overjoyed to see him. I felt friendship for him, and tenderness. But when he wasn't there, I did not miss him. Such was the equation of my feeling for him, and I thought it was a marvelous story.

That is why I dreaded his declarations, for they seemed to demand a response or, worse yet, some reciprocity. To tell lies at this level is torture. Then I discovered that my fears were not justified: Rinri expected nothing more than that I listen. How right he was! It is a huge thing in and of itself to listen to someone. And I listened fervently.

There was no name for what I felt for this boy in modern French, but this was not the case in Japanese, where the term *koi* was most appropriate. *Koi,* in classical French, might be translated by *goût,* liking. He was to my liking. He was my *koibito,* the man with whom I shared the *koi*: his company was to my liking.

In modern Japanese, young couples who are not married qualify their partners as *koibito.* Visceral modesty banishes the word love. Unless it is by accident, or in a fit of delirious passion, this enormous word is not to be used, as it is reserved for literature and that sort of thing. As luck would have it I had chanced on the only Japanese man who had no such disdain for the vocabulary or for spontaneous behavior. But I reassured myself with the thought that linguistic exoticism must have played a significant role in this bizarre state of affairs. The fact that Rinri's declarations were directed to a French-speaking woman and could be uttered in either French or in Japanese surely had something to do with it: the French language, no doubt, represented a territory that was both prestigious and licentious, a place where one could indulge one's inadmissible feelings.

Love is such a very French élan that there are some who view it as a national invention. While I would not go that far, I do acknowledge that there is a genius for love in the language. It might be said that Rinri and I had each contracted the typical inclination of the other's language: giddy with the novelty of it, he played at love, and I delighted in *koi.* Which all goes to show how admirably open we were to each other's culture.

There was only one thing wrong with *koi:* the name. It is the exact homonym of carp, the only beast that has ever filled me with repulsion. Fortunately, there was no resemblance between the fish and my feeling: even if a carp, in Japan, can symbolize a boy, the feelings I had for Rinri in no way evoked the large slimy fish with the disgusting mouth. On the contrary, *koi* was ravishing, so light, fluid, fresh and devoid of seriousness. *Koi* was elegant, playful, funny, civilized. One of the charms of *koi* lay in the opportunities it offered for parodying love: certain attitudes of love could be adopted not to criticize but rather to provide an honest source of fun.

I did, however, strive to hide my mirth in order not to hurt Rinri; love's lack of a sense of humor is notorious. I suspect that he already knew that what I felt for him was *koi* and not *ai*—a word so beautiful that I did on occasion regret I could not use it. If Rinri did not express any sadness over the fact, it was no doubt out of a sense of inaugural consciousness: he must have understood that he was my first *koi*, just as I was his first love. For while I may have burned with desire on numerous occasions, I had never found someone who was to my liking.

Between the two words, *koi* and *ai*, there is no variation of intensity, but an essential incompatibility. Can one fall in love with a person one has a liking for? Unthinkable. One falls in love with a person one cannot stand, a person who represents an unbearable danger. Schopenhauer saw in love the ruses of our reproductive instincts: I cannot express the horror this theory inspires in me. I see, in love, the ruses of my instinct not to assassinate another person: when I feel the need to kill a specific individual, some mysterious mechanism—an immune reflex? phantasm of innocence? fear of being sent to jail?—causes me to crystallize around that person. And so it has transpired that, to the best of my knowledge, I have, to date, never murdered a soul.

Murder Rinri? What an atrocious and above all absurd idea! Murder someone so sweet, who has never inspired in me anything but the best intentions! And anyway, I did not kill him, which is proof that it was not necessary.

There is nothing banal about the fact that I'm writing a story where no one wants to massacre anyone. That's what a story about *koi* must be all about.

Rinri was the one who prepared our meals. He was not a good cook, but he was better than I was—a fact which holds true for all of humankind. It would have been a pity to let all of Christine's magnificent household appliances go to waste. He served up some dubious pasta dishes he dubbed *carbonara*—his interpretation of this classic was to incorporate every variety of fat on the planet in 1989, and in abundance. Japanese cuisine is very light, it's a well-known fact. In this domain, too, I cannot exclude the hypothesis that I was the pretext for a loosening of cultural constraints.

Instead of informing him that his dish was inedible, I spoke to him of my passion for sashimi and sushi. He made a face.

"Don't you like it?" I asked.

"Yes, yes," he said politely.

"It must be very difficult to prepare."

"Yes."

"You could buy some from a delicatessen."

"Do you really want me to?"

"Why do you say you like it if you don't?"

"I do like it. But when I eat food like that, it's as if I'm at a family dinner and my grandparents are there."

A valid point.

"And moreover, when I eat it with them, they go on and on about how it's good for your health. That's boring," he added.

"I see. So it makes you feel like eating things that are bad for your health, like spaghetti carbonara," I said.

"Is it bad for your health?"

"Your version undoubtedly is."

"That's precisely why it's delicious."

Now it was going to be even more difficult to ask him to prepare something else.

"Or I could make us another fondue?" he suggested.

"No."

"Didn't you like it?"

"Yes, but it's such a special memory. If you make it again, we will only be disappointed."

Phew. I had found a polite excuse.

"What about the *okonomiyaki* we had at your friends' place?" I suggested.

"Yes, that's easy."

Saved. It became our own special meal. The fridge was constantly filled with shrimp, eggs, cabbage and ginger. A carton of plum sauce reigned over the table.

"Where do you buy this delicious sauce?" I asked.

"I have a supply at home. My parents brought it back from Hiroshima."

"Which means that when you run out, you'll have to go back there."

"I've never been there."

"Good. You saw nothing in Hiroshima. Nothing."

"Why do you say that?"

I explained that it was a parody of a classic of French cinéma littéraire.

"I didn't see that film," he said, indignant.

"You can read the book."

"What's the story about?"

"I'd prefer not to tell you and let you find out."

In all that time spent together, we hardly left the apartment. Christine's return was rapidly approaching, and we viewed with terror our departure from this place that had played such a significant role in our affair.

"We could barricade the door," I suggested.

"Would you do that?" he asked, with awestruck admiration.

I loved to think he believed me capable of such evil-doing.

We spent an inordinate amount of time in the bathroom. The bathtub was the size of a hollowed-out whale with its blowhole directed inward.

Rinri, respectful of tradition, scrubbed himself all over at the sink before getting into the bath: one must not sully the waters of the honorable bathtub. I could not comply with a custom I found absurd. One might as well put clean dishes into a dishwasher.

I explained my point of view to him.

"Perhaps you are right," he said, "but I can't do it any other way. To defile the bath water is too much for me."

"Whereas uttering blasphemy about Japanese food is not a problem for you."

"That's just the way it is."

He was right. We all have our reactionary strongholds, it's not something you can explain.

In the whale-bath I sometimes felt we were sinking, being drawn down to the bottom of the ocean.

"You know the story of Jonah?" I asked.

"Don't talk about whales. We'll get into an argument."

"Don't tell me you're one of those Japanese who eat whale meat?"

"I know it's wrong. It's not my fault it tastes so good."

"I've tasted it, it's revolting!"

"You see? If you'd liked it, you wouldn't think there was anything shocking about our habits."

"But whales are becoming extinct!"

"I know. We are wrong. What do you want? When I think of the taste of the meat, my mouth waters. I can't help it."

He was not typically Japanese. For example, he had traveled a great deal—and always alone, without a camera.

"It's something I hide from other people. If my parents had known I was going away on my own, they would have been worried."

"Would they have thought you were in danger?"

"No. They would have worried about my mental health. Here, if you like traveling without company, you're crazy. In our language, the word 'alone' contains the notion of despair."

"But you have some famous hermits in this country."

"Exactly. People think that in order to appreciate solitude you have to be a bonze."

"Why is it that your compatriots always go around in a group when they're abroad, more than they ever do at home?"

"They like to see people who are different from them but at the same time they want to be reassured by the presence of people just like them."

"And this need to take photos of everything?"

"I don't know. It's so annoying, especially as they all take identical photos. Maybe it's to prove to themselves that they haven't been dreaming."

"I've never seen you with a camera."

"I don't have one."

"You've got every single gadget that exists, including a burner for eating cheese fondue in a spaceship, and you don't have a camera?"

"No. It doesn't interest me."

"Good old Rinri."

He asked me what I meant by that expression. I explained it to him. He found it so strange that he began saying it twenty times a day: "Good old Amélie."

One afternoon there was a sudden downpour, followed by a hailstorm. I watched the spectacle from the window and remarked, "So you have cloudbursts in Japan too."

Behind me I heard his voice echoing, "Cloudburst."

I realized this was a new word for him, that the context had specified the meaning to him, and now he was saying it to print it on his memory. I laughed. He seemed to understand why I was amused so he said, "Good old me."

Christine came back from Belgium at the beginning of April. Out of the goodness of my heart I gave the apartment back to her. Rinri seemed more devastated than I did. Our affair had to take a more erratic course. I was not totally displeased with this. I had been missing our monophyly somewhat.

I went back to the concrete château. Rinri's parents no longer called me Sensei, which confirmed their perspicacity. His grandparents called me Sensei more than ever, which confirmed their perversity.

One day while I was having tea with all these good people, the father showed me a piece of jewelry he had just designed. It was a bizarre necklace, halfway between a mobile by Calder and an onyx rivière.

"Do you like it?" he asked.

"I like the way the black and silver go together. Very elegant."

"It belongs to you."

Rinri fastened it around my neck. I was very touched. When I was alone with him I said, "You father has given me a magnificent present. How can I ever repay him?"

"If you give him something, he'll give you even more."

"What must I do?"

"Nothing."

He was right. To avoid ever-increasing displays of generosity, there is no other solution than to bravely accept such lavish offerings.

In the meantime I had moved back into my humble abode. Rinri was too tactful to ask me to take him there, but he did drop hints, which I painstakingly ignored.

He called frequently. He expressed himself in an unintentionally comical way that was delightful, particularly as he was utterly serious:

"Hello Amélie. I am calling to inquire about the state of your health."

"Excellent."

"Since that is the case, do you wish to see me?"

I burst out laughing. He could not understand why.

Rinri had a younger sister who was eighteen and who was studying in Los Angeles. One day he informed me that she was coming to Tokyo for a short vacation.

"I'll come and fetch you this evening so you can meet her."

His voice trembled with solemn emotion. I prepared myself to experience something important.

When I had climbed into the Mercedes, I turned around to greet the young woman sitting on the back seat. Her beauty astounded me.

"Amélie, this is Rika. Rika, this is Amélie."

She greeted me with an exquisite smile. Her name was a disappointment, but not the rest. She was an angel.

"Rinri has talked a lot about you," she said.

"He has talked a lot about you, too," I invented.

"You're both lying. I never talk a lot."

"That's true, he never says a thing," continued Rika. "He has hardly said a thing about you. That is why I am convinced he loves you."

"In that case he loves you, too."

"I hope you don't mind if I speak to you in English? I make too many mistakes in Japanese."

"I'm not the one who would notice them."

"Rinri is forever correcting me. He wants me to be perfect."

She was beyond perfection. The young man took us to Shirogane park. At nightfall the place was so deserted that it felt as if we were far away from Tokyo, in some mythical forest.

Rika got out of the car carrying a bag which she then opened. She pulled out a silk tablecloth which she spread on the ground, then some saké, glasses, and cakes. She sat on the cloth and invited us to do likewise. Her grace dazzled me.

While we were toasting our acquaintance, I asked her which ideograms went to make up her first name. She showed me.

"The land of perfume!" I exclaimed. "That's marvelous, and it suits you perfectly."

Now that I knew the meaning in Japanese, her first name no longer seemed ugly.

Life in California had made her more communicative than her brother. She babbled away in a charming manner. I lapped up her words. Rinri seemed to be as hypnotized as I was. We contemplated her as if she were some ravishing natural phenomenon.

"Okay," she said suddenly. "What about those fireworks, then?"

"I'll see to it," said the boy.

I was flabbergasted. Rinri removed a suitcase from the trunk, which turned out to be the fireworks suitcase, just as there had been the Swiss-cheese fondue suitcase. He laid out his pyrotechnician's gear on the ground, and warned us that he was about to begin. Soon the sky above showered us with explosions of colors and stars, echoed by the young woman's ecstatic cries.

Before my dazzled eyes, a brother was offering his sister not the proof but the expression of his love. Never had I felt so close to him.

When the aurora borealis had ceased crackling above our heads, Rika exclaimed with disappointment, "Is it over already?"

"There are still some sparklers," said Rinri.

He took a bundle of twigs from the suitcase and gave a handful to each of us. He lit only one at a time, which then spread the blaze to all the others. Each little stick crackled with a cluster of swirling sparks.

Night silvered the bamboo in Shirogane park. Our apocalypse of fireflies projected its gold glow onto the matte white backdrop. Brother and sister gazed with wonder at their starry wands. I realized I was in the presence of two children who were smitten with each other, and I was deeply moved at the sight of it.

What a gift, to be allowed to share their company! It was more than an expression of love: it was an expression of trust.

The cotton-candy wisps of light finally went out, but the spell was not broken. Rika sighed with joy. "That was great."

I shared Rinri's love for this happy little child. Here was a dreamy, romantic atmosphere, replete with the young girl of legends at a crepuscular celebration. Gérard de Nerval in Japan, who would have thought!

The following evening Rinri took me to eat Chinese noodles at a greasy spoon.

"I adore your sister," I said.

"I do, too," he replied, with a tender smile.

"You know, we have a strange thing in common, you and I. I adore my sister, too, and she also lives far away. Her name is Juliette, and it cost me a superhuman effort to leave her."

I showed him a photo of my sacred older sister.

"She's beautiful," he remarked, looking at her attentively.

"Yes, and she's more than just beautiful. I miss her."

"I understand. When Rika is in California I miss her terribly."

Over my bowl I waxed elegiac. I told him that he alone could understand how bereft I felt in Juliette's absence. I told him how strong the bond between us had always been, how much I loved her, and how I had wrought an absurd violence upon myself by leaving her behind.

"I had to come back to Japan, but did I have to experience such a wrenching separation?"

"Why didn't she come with you?"

"She wants to live in Belgium, where she has her work. She doesn't share my passion for your country."

"Like Rika. Japan is not the country of her dreams."

How was it possible that two creatures as delightful as our own sisters could fail to be fascinated by Japan? I asked Rinri what Rika was studying in California. He replied that her program was very vague, that in actual fact she was the mistress of a certain Chang, a Chinese man who reigned over the Los Angeles underworld.

"You cannot imagine how rich he is," he said, with amused despair.

I was dumbfounded. How on earth could this angel from heaven have ended up living with a mob boss? "Don't be so stupid," I said to myself, "this has always been the way of the world." In my mind I suddenly saw Rika, feather boa around her neck and in high heels, walking arm-in-arm with a Chinese man in a white suit. I burst out laughing.

Rinri gave me a knowing smile. Our respective sisters appeared in the broth of our noodles. Our affair had meaning.

I was thrilled by my progress in Japanese—although it was not as great as Rinri's progress in French, which was dazzling. We played at trying to out-impress each other with our linguistic prowess. One day when it was pouring, Rinri said, "It's pissing it down."

Which, coming from his ever distinguished voice, had a certain comic effect.

When he said something utterly outrageous, I would burst out with, "*Nani o shaimasu ka?*"

Which can be translated—or rather cannot be translated, because no one but the Japanese would use a turn of phrase so aristocratic that even they no longer use it—as: "What dare you to utter so honorably?"

He collapsed with laughter. One evening his parents had invited me to have dinner at their concrete château, and I wanted to impress them. The moment Rinri said something surprising, I declared for all to hear, "*Nani o shaimasu ka?*"

Once their initial astonishment had waned, Rinri's father howled with laughter. The grandparents were indignant and told me off, alleging that I had no right to say such a thing. Rinri's mother waited for silence to return, then declared with a smile, "Why do you go to so much bother to act distinguished when it's obvious that with such an expressive face you will never be a lady?"

This served to confirm what her politeness had already suggested: she despised me. Not only was I stealing her son from her, I was a foreigner. And in addition to these two crimes, she seemed to suspect me of something else that was even more hateful to her.

"If Rika were here, she would have laughed until she cried," said Rinri, who had not noticed his mother's nasty remark.

In the past I had learned English, Dutch, German and Italian. There was one similar feature to all these living languages: I could understand them better than I could speak them. This was perfectly logical: you observe behavior before you adopt it. Linguistic intuition operates even when competency has not yet been attained.

In Japanese, it was the other way around: my active knowledge far surpassed my passive knowledge. This phenomenon has never abated and I cannot explain it. On numerous occasions I was able to express in Japanese ideas that were so sophisticated that the person I was speaking to thought they were dealing with a professor of Japanese studies, and would reply in terms of a comparably lofty level of language. All that was left for me to do was to flee if I wanted to hide the fact that I had not grasped a single word of what he or she had said. When a hasty retreat was out of the question, I could only imagine what the person opposite me might have said, and carry on with my monologue disguised as dialogue.

I expounded on the phenomenon to linguists, who assured me that this was normal: "It is impossible to have linguistic intuition in a language that is so far removed from your own." That failed to take into account the fact that I spoke Japanese until I was five years old. Moreover, I had lived in China, Bangladesh, and other such places, and there, as elsewhere, my passive knowledge of the language prevailed over my active. Thus in my case there is truly a Japanese exception, and I am tempted to explain it by destiny: in Japan, for me to be passive was unthinkable.

*

What was bound to happen happened: in June, Rinri announced with funereal gloom that we had run out of bitter plum sauce.

"The way we were going through it, it could hardly have been otherwise."

His progress in French fascinated me. I replied, "So much the better! I've been dreaming of going to Hiroshima with you."

His face went from grave to terrible. I sought an historical explanation and parleyed, "The entire world admired the courage with which Hiroshima and Nagasaki endured . . ."

"That has nothing to do with it," he interrupted. "I read that little book written by a Frenchwoman, the one you mentioned to me—"

"*Hiroshima mon amour.*"

"Yes. I didn't understand a thing."

I burst out laughing.

"Don't worry, a lot of French-speaking people have had the same experience. All the more reason to go to Hiroshima," I improvised.

"You mean that if you read the book in Hiroshima you understand it?"

"I'm sure," I decreed.

"That's utter nonsense. I don't need to go to Venice to understand *Death in Venice* or to Parma to read *The Charterhouse of Parma.*"

"Marguerite Duras is a very particular author," I said, convinced that what I said was true.

We arranged to meet the following Saturday at seven in the morning at Haneda airport. I would have preferred to travel by train but for the Japanese the train is such an everyday experience that Rinri needed a change.

"Also, flying over Hiroshima must give the impression of being on board the Enola Gay," he said.

It was the beginning of June. The weather in Tokyo was ideal: clear, twenty-five degrees. In Hiroshima it was five degrees warmer and the humidity of the rainy season had already begun to linger in the air. But the sun was there for us.

From the moment we landed in Hiroshima I had the overwhelming and singular impression that this was not 1989. I no longer knew what year it was—not 1945, to be sure, but something not unlike the fifties or sixties. Had the atomic blast slowed the movement of time? There was no lack of modern architecture, people were dressed normally, the cars were no different from those anywhere in Japan. It was as if people were living more intensely here than elsewhere. Living in a city whose very name symbolized death to the entire planet had exalted their living fiber; this in turn led to an impression of optimism, which recreated the atmosphere of an era where people still believed in the future.

This thought affected me deeply. I was immediately taken with the city, with its heart-wrenching atmosphere of courageous happiness.

The Atomic Bomb Museum was astonishing. However much you might think you know, the details defy imagination. Events are presented with a precision that borders on poetry: there is the train which, on August 6, 1945, was on its way up the coast toward Hiroshima with its carriages full of the morning's workers. Passengers were gazing dozily out the window at the city through the carriage windows. Then the train entered a tunnel and when it came out again, the workers saw that Hiroshima was gone.

I reflected that the most striking illustration of Japanese dignity was to be found here, in the streets of this provincial town. There was nothing, absolutely nothing, to suggest its martyrdom. It seemed to me that in any other country a monstrous event of such huge proportions would have been exploited to the hilt. Capital of victimization, national treasure of so many nations—in Hiroshima this did not exist.

In the Peace Park lovers kissed timidly on public benches. I suddenly recalled that I was not alone, and complied with local custom. When this was done, Rinri pulled a copy of *Hiroshima mon amour* from his pocket. I'd forgotten all about it; he could think of nothing else. He read it out loud, from beginning to end.

It was as if he were reading out my indictment, and I would be held accountable for everything he reproached me with. The text was long, and his Japanese accent slowed it down even further, so I had time to prepare my defense. The hardest thing was to keep from laughing when, irritated by his failure to understand, he read, "You kill me, you are good for me." He didn't say it the way Emmanuelle Riva did.

Two hours later, when he had finished, he closed the book and looked at me.

"It's magnificent, isn't it?" I dared to murmur.

"I don't know," he replied, implacable.

I was not about to get off so lightly.

"To take a young French woman who had her head shaved when Liberation came, and the population of Hiroshima, and place them on the same level—you have to have the nerve of someone like Duras to get away with it."

"Oh, really? Is that what it means?" asked Rinri.

"Yes. It is a book that exalts love as the victim of barbarity."

"Why does the author say it in such an odd way?"

"That's Marguerite Duras. The charm of it is that you feel things without necessarily understanding them."

"But I didn't feel anything."

"Yes you did, you were angry."

"That's how she wants you to react?"

"It's what she likes, it's the right attitude. When you finish one of her books you go away feeling frustrated. It's as if there's been an interrogation where very little was made clear. You've glimpsed things through frosted glass. You leave the dinner table and you're still hungry."

"I'm hungry."

"So am I."

Okonomiyaki is the specialty of Hiroshima. They serve it at huge open air dives, on gigantic griddles spewing smoke out into the night. Although it was relatively cool that evening, the cook was sweating profusely into the cabbage pancake he was preparing before our eyes. Drops of sweat contributed to the masterpiece. Never had we eaten such delectable *okonomiyaki*. Rinri took the opportunity to buy a prodigious number of boxes of sour plum sauce from the chef.

After that, the hotel room offered me the pretext to declaim a few phrases of my own from Duras's book. Rinri seemed to appreciate them more this time around. It would be impossible to overstate how fervently I devoted myself to the cause of French literature.

At the beginning of July, my sister came to join me for a month of vacation. I thought I would die of joy when I saw her. For an hour our hugs were nothing but a series of animal grunts and squeals.

That evening, Rinri was waiting outside my house in the white Mercedes. I introduced him to the person who was most precious to me in the world. They were both dreadfully intimidated. It was up to me to make conversation.

Once I was alone again with Juliette, I asked her what she thought of Rinri.

"He's thin," she said.

"But what else?"

I couldn't get much else out of her. Then I phoned Rinri.

"So, how do you find her?"

"She's thin," he said.

I couldn't get much else out of him. Beyond the hypothesis of a setup, I felt deeply indignant: such poor judgment! Yes of course they were thin—and so what? Didn't they have anything more interesting to say to me? What I found most striking in each of them was certainly not their thinness: in my sister, it was her beauty and magic; in Rinri, his thoughtfulness and eccentricity.

Yet there was nothing hostile about their reciprocal observation: they liked each other from the start. With hindsight, I can see they were right. If I look back over my past, I note that absolutely all of the people who have played an important role in my life have been thin. While obviously this is not their principal characteristic, it is the one point they all have in common. It must mean something.

To be sure, along the way I have encountered other manifestations of thinness that in no way changed the course of my destiny. Moreover I have lived in Bangladesh, where the majority of the population are skin and bone: one life alone cannot incorporate so many others, even if they are skinny. But on my deathbed, the figures parading through my memory will all be as lean as they come.

So although I am unaware of the significance this may entail, I do suspect it is a personal choice, whether conscious or not. In my novels, objects of affection are always extremely slim. But nor should one conclude that this is all that matters to me. Two years ago a silly little goose whose identity I shall not disclose came and offered herself to me in a capacity that I prefer not to think about. When said goose saw my dismay, she twirled before me in order to emphasize her svelte person and declared—and this I swear—"Don't you think I look just like one of your heroines?"

Back to the summer of 1989. I dismissed my thin young lover for a month: Juliette and I were setting off on our pilgrimage.

We traveled by train to Kansai. The province was as beautiful as ever. And yet I would not wish such a journey on anyone. It is a miracle that I survived such a heart-breaking experience. Had my sister not been there, I should never have had the courage to return to the place of our childhood. Had my sister not been there, I should have died of sorrow in the village of Shukugawa.

On August 5, Juliette went back to Belgium. I shut myself away for several hours to howl like a beast. When my chest was empty of every sob it contained, I called Rinri. He was kind enough to hide his joy, for he knew how I was suffering. The white Mercedes came to fetch me.

We drove to Shirogane park.

"The last time we came here was with Rika," I said. "Did you make use of our time apart to go and see her?"

"No. She's not the same, over there. She puts on an act."

"So what did you do?"

"I read a book in French about the Knights of the Order of the Temple," he declared, with exaltation.

"That's nice."

"Yes, and I've decided to become one of them."

"I don't understand."

"I want to become a Templar."

I spent the rest of our walk explaining to Rinri the untimeliness of his ambition. Under King Philip IV, in Europe, it might have made sense. In Tokyo in 1989, coming from the future director of a renowned jewelry school, it was absurd.

"I want to become a Templar," insisted Rinri, crushed. "I am sure there is already an order of the Temple in Japan."

"I'm sure there is, too, given that there is already everything else in your country. Your compatriots are so curious that whatever your passion might be you always find someone to share it with."

"Why shouldn't I become a Templar?"

"Nowadays it seems rather like a sect."

He sighed, defeated.

"Why don't we go eat some Chinese noodles?" my aspiring knight Templar eventually suggested.

"Excellent idea."

During the meal, I tried to tell him the story of *The Accursed Kings*. The hardest thing to explain was the Pope's election.

"It hasn't changed at all. The cardinals still meet in conclave, shut off by themselves . . ."

I got carried away and spared no detail. He listened, sucking up his noodles. When I had finished my presentation, I asked, "What do they think of the Pope in Japan, actually?"

Usually when I would ask Rinri a question, he would pause and reflect before replying. This time he did not reflect for an instant but said, "Nothing."

It was uttered in such a neutral voice that I burst out laughing. There was no insolence in his definitive tone, merely a statement of fact.

Since then, whenever I see a Pope on the television, I muse, "And here is this man about whom twenty-five million Japanese think nothing"—and the mere thought of it always makes me feel like laughing.

Besides, given how curious the Japanese are about all things foreign, it is almost certain that Rinri's reply allowed room for numerous exceptions. But I believe I was right to dissuade him from joining the Knights Templar, given that he showed so little interest in his principal enemy.

I 'm taking you to the mountains tomorrow," announced Rinri on the phone. "Put on your hiking boots."

"Maybe it's not a good idea."

"Why not? Don't you like the mountains?"

"I'm in love with the mountains."

"So, that's settled," he decided, indifferent to my paradoxes.

No sooner had he hung up than I felt the fever rising in me: mountains the world over, and therefore all the more so in Japan, exert an almost alarming attraction over me. I knew however that the adventure would not be without a certain amount of risk: above one thousand five hundred meters in altitude I become another person.

On August 11 the white Mercedes opened its door to me.

"Where are we going?"

"You'll see."

Although I've never been good at ideograms, I have always been able to read place names. This gracious exception has been extremely useful in the course of my Japanese voyages. After a very long drive my suspicion was confirmed: "Mount Fuji!"

My dream. Tradition holds that all Japanese people must climb Mount Fuji at least once in their life, for otherwise they do not deserve their prestigious nationality. For me, with my fervent desire to become Japanese, the climb afforded a marvelously clever access to identity. All the more so as mountains are my territory, my terrain.

Rinri parked in a gigantic lot on the lava plain, beyond which no cars were allowed. The profusion of tourist buses was impressive, confirming how greatly people needed to obtain their title of True Japanese. There was nothing official about it: the idea was simply to go from sea level to an altitude of 3,776 meters in less than a day, since only the base and the summit offered any sort of accommodation for an overnight stay. And among the crowd gathered at the start of the climb were old people, children, mothers carrying babies—I even saw a pregnant woman who must have been in her eighth month. Which goes to show that Japanese nationality always has a heroic connotation.

I looked above me: so this was Mount Fuji. At last I had found a place where the Mount seemed less magnificent, for the simple reason that the mountain itself is not visible from the base. The volcano is a sublime invention that you can see from almost everywhere, so much so that at times I took it for a hologram. I've lost count of the number of places on Honshu that offer a superb view of Mount Fuji: it would be easier to count the number of places from which you cannot see it. If nationalists had wanted to create a unifying symbol, they would have had to build Mount Fuji. It is impossible to gaze at it without feeling a sacred, mythical tingling: it is too beautiful, too perfect, too ideal.

Except at the foot, where it resembled any old mountain, a sort of shapeless lump.

Rinri had his equipment: mountaineering boots, a space suit fit for sidereal exploration, and an ice axe. He looked at my sneakers and jeans with commiseration but refrained from making any comments, perhaps in order not to rub salt in the wound.

"Shall we go?" he asked.

That was what I was waiting for. I let my legs loose, and they took off. The sun was at its zenith and so was my spirit. I was

climbing, and happy to have so much to climb. The first fifteen
hundred meters were the hardest: the ground was nothing but
soft lava into which my feet sank. You have to really want to do
it. We all wanted to. The sight of the little old people climbing
one behind the other obliged us to feel full of respect.

Once we were above fifteen hundred meters it became real
mountain terrain, with masses of rock and hard earth, surrounded by areas of loose black shale. I had reached the altitude where I change species. I waited for Rinri, who was only
two hundred meters behind me, and I told him to meet me at
the summit.

Later, he would say, "I don't know what happened after
that. You vanished."

He was right. Above fifteen hundred meters, I vanish. My
body is transformed into pure energy, and by the time people
wonder where I've gone to, my legs have taken me so far away
that I become invisible. Others may have this facility, but I
know no one of whom you would suspect it so little, for however you look at it, I do not resemble Zarathustra.

But that is who I become. A superhuman strength takes over
and I make a beeline for the sun. My brain echoes with
anthems—not Olympic, but rather Olympian anthems. Hercules
is my puny little cousin. And that's only the Greek side of the
family. We Zoroastrians are another thing altogether.

To be Zarathustra is to have, for feet, gods who devour the
mountain and transform it into sky, and for knees, catapults
that turn your body into a projectile. For a stomach you have
a war drum, and for a heart, a triumphant beating percussion;
in your brain there dwells such formidable joy that you must
have a superhuman strength to bear it; you possess every
power on the earth; you have invoked these powers and you
can contain them all in your blood; you will never touch the
earth again, for you are absorbed in a close dialogue with the
sun.

Fate, renowned for its sense of humor, decreed that I should be born Belgian. To be born a child of the flatlands when you belong to the Zoroastrian lineage: someone up there has thumbed their nose at you, condemning you to the life of a double agent.

I overtook hordes of Japanese. Some looked up from the ground to stare at the meteor. The old men said, "*Wakaimono*," ("young thing"), as if that were an explanation. As for the other young people, they could find nothing to say.

When I had overtaken all the hikers, I saw that I was not alone. Among the day's climbers was another Zarathustra, and he absolutely insisted upon making my acquaintance: an American GI from the base at Okinawa, who had come to have a look around.

"I was beginning to believe I was abnormal," he said to me, "but you're a girl and you're climbing just like me."

I did not want to explain to him that from time immemorial there have always been female Zoroastrians. He did not deserve to belong to the lineage: he was talkative and indifferent to what was holy. All families have this type of hereditary defect.

The landscape was becoming sublime, and I tried to open the eyes of my American cousin onto such splendor. All he could find to say was, "Yeah, great country."

I divined that he would have shown equal enthusiasm for a plateful of pancakes.

I tried to get rid of him by moving up to a higher gear. Alas, he stuck right behind me, saying over and over, "That a girl!"

He was friendly, that is, not the least bit Zoroastrian. I dreamt of regaining my solitude in order to discover the sort of Zoroastrian-Wagnerian-Nietzschean frame of mind that would be appropriate for the situation. Impossible, with this GI chattering nonstop and asking me if Belgium was the place all those tulips were from. Never had I cursed the American military presence in Okinawa to such a degree.

At three thousand five hundred meters I asked him politely to keep quiet, explaining that this was a sacred mountain and that I wanted to climb the remaining two hundred and seventy six meters in a mood of contemplation. "No problem," said he. I managed to extricate myself from his company and, intoxicated, I finished the ascent.

At the summit was the moon, an immense stone circumference surrounding the abyss of the crater. You could only keep your balance if you walked along the disc. If you turned around, there beneath the blue sky was the Japanese plain, as far as the eye could see.

It was four o'clock in the afternoon.

"What are you going to do now?" asked the GI.

"I'll wait for my boyfriend."

My answer had the desired effect: the American immediately set off again for the plain. I sighed with pleasure.

I strolled along the edge of the crater. It would take an entire day, I wagered, to walk the entire circumference. No one would dare venture into the center: the volcano may be extinct, but this giants' quarry was haunted by holiness.

I sat on the ground, facing the spot where the pilgrims would arrive. Everyone climbed up the same slope of the mountain, though I could not see why, given the fact that it was conical. Perhaps it was solely by virtue of some sort of Japanese conformism—something that I too had adhered to, since I wanted to be Japanese. Apart from the American man and myself, I could see no foreigners. It was touching to watch as the old people arrived at the summit, leaning on their walking sticks, very dignified, yet delighted with their exploit.

One eighty-year-old man, who arrived at around six o'clock, cried out, "Now I am a Japanese citizen worthy of the name!"

Thus, the war had not sufficed to confer knighthood. Only a difference in altitude of 3,776 meters gave the right to the title.

In any other country, where the population was less honest,

so many people would have fraudulently laid claim to the ascent that an office distributing certificates would have to be erected at the edge of the crater. I would have liked such an arrangement. Alas, I would have nothing more at my disposal than my word of honor to vouch for my accomplishment: and no doubt it would be of little purpose.

Rinri did not arrive until six-thirty.

"You were here!" he exclaimed, relieved.

"For ages."

He collapsed on the ground.

"I can't take another step."

"So, you're truly Japanese now."

"As if this was what I needed to become truly Japanese!"

I noted this difference in point of view from the old man's half an hour earlier. Nationality seemed to have lost a great deal of its prestige in the interim.

"You're not going to stay there, are you?" I asked.

And I yanked him to his feet to lead him to the long lodge where we could have some bunks for the night. Rinri offered me some cookies and fluorescent soda, and I reminded him that we would have to wake before dawn to watch the sunrise.

"How did you get up here so quickly?" he asked.

"It's because I'm Zarathustra," I replied.

"Zarathustra. The one who thus spake?"

"Exactly."

Rinri registered the information without surprise, and fell asleep. I shook him to wake him up, I wanted his company. Might as well tickle a dead man. How could I possibly feel sleepy? I was at the top of Mount Fuji, this was far too impressive for me to waste time sleeping. I went out of the lodge.

Night had flooded the plain. In the distance you could see a vast luminous mushroom: Tokyo. I was trembling with cold and the emotion of having this encapsulated vision of Japan before my eyes: ancient Fuji, and the futuristic capital.

I lay down craterwise and spent my insomnia shivering with ideas so much greater than I. Everyone at the lodge had eventually fallen asleep. I wanted to be the one who would see the first light of day.

While I waited, I was witness to an extraordinary sight. After midnight, luminous processions began to climb the mountain. Apparently, there were people courageous enough to attempt the ascent at night, no doubt to avoid spending too much time waiting for sunrise in the cold air. For no one should miss the ceremony of the sunrise. It did not matter if you arrived early. With tears in my eyes I watched these slow golden caterpillars meandering their way toward the summit. There could be no doubt that they were not athletes but ordinary people. How could you fail to admire such a nation?

At around four in the morning, just as the first nocturnal walkers were arriving, filaments of light appeared in the sky. I went to shake Rinri, who grumbled that he was already Japanese and that he would meet me at the car at the end of the day. I thought that if I deserved to be Japanese, he deserved to be Belgian, and I went back outside. People were beginning to gather, to look out at the dawning of the day.

I joined the group. We stood watching for the star in the deepest of silences. My heart began to pound. Not a cloud in the summer sky. Behind us, the abyss of the dead volcano.

Suddenly, a red fragment appeared on the horizon. A shiver ran through the silent assembly. And then, with a speed that did not preclude majesty, the entire disc rose from nothingness and overlooked the plain.

Something happened in that instant, and the memory of it continues to move me to this day: from the throats of the hundreds of people gathered there, including my own, rose the cry, "*Banzai!*"

It was an understatement: ten thousand years could not

have sufficed to express the sense of Japanese eternity that the sight aroused.

We must have resembled a rally of extreme right-wingers. And yet the good folk who were gathered there were surely no more fascist than you or I. In actual fact, we were partaking not of an ideology but of a mythology, and surely it was one of the most cogent on the planet.

My eyes welling with tears, I watched as the Japanese flag gradually lost its red, spilling gold into the still bleary azure. And I felt happier than a queen.

When the collective ecstasy had abated somewhat, I heard a fellow say, "We have to go back down now. I think that's harder than going up. Apparently the record for the descent is fifty-five minutes. I wonder how that can be possible, especially when you consider that you're eliminated if you fall: you have to stay on your feet the entire time."

"That seems self-evident," said someone else.

"Not at all. The ground is so slippery that you could go down in a seated position. I saw an old lady do it."

"You mean that this isn't the first time you've climbed?"

"It's my third climb. I can't get enough."

He deserved Japanese nationality several times over, I thought. And his words had not fallen on the ears of a deaf woman.

I stood facing the sun, and at five-thirty exactly I flung myself onto the slope. I had removed my brakes. What I experienced was beyond grandiose: in order not to fall, I had to keep my legs in constant motion, running through the lava, moving my brain as quickly as my feet, never allowing for one second my madness to interrupt my vigilance, laughing to keep from falling whenever, inevitably, I began to slide down the slope, thus accelerating my rhythm; I was a hurtling meteor beneath the rising sun, I was my own subject for ballistic studies, I was shouting fit to wake the volcano.

When I reached the parking lot, it was not yet six fifteen: I had broken the record, and by a considerable amount. Alas, there was no way I could make it official. My exploit would never be anything more than a personal myth.

I found a faucet where I was able to quench my thirst and wash the splatters of lava from my face. All that was left to do now was to wait for Rinri. It seemed it might take quite a while. Fortunately it is impossible to be bored when you can observe a procession of human beings, particularly in Japan. I sat on the ground, and for hours I contemplated the people I now considered to be my virtual compatriots.

It must have been two in the afternoon when Rinri came to join me. He seemed to be held together with spare parts. Uncomplainingly, he drove me back to Tokyo in the Mercedes.

The next morning a delivery arrived with twenty-two red roses. There was an accompanying note: "Dear Zarathustra, Happy Birthday!" He apologized for not being the superman who could have brought them to me in person. His pain-wracked legs could no longer carry him.

A few days later Rinri called to tell me that his family had gone away on a trip for a week. He begged me to move in with him for the duration.

I accepted with equal amounts of curiosity and apprehension: I had never spent so much time constantly in his company.

He came to fetch me and my bundle of belongings. When we arrived at the concrete château I asked, very intimidated, "Where will I sleep?"

"With me, in my parents' bed."

I protested against such a breach of propriety. Rinri responded with his usual shrug of the shoulders.

"Your parents' bed—what are you thinking!"

"As long as they aren't aware of it," he said.

"Well, I will be aware of it!"

"You don't really want us to sleep together in my tiny single bed? It would be hell."

"Is there no other possibility?"

"Yes. We can sleep in my grandparents' bed."

His reasoning struck home. Given the disgust his grandparents inspired in me, I relented with relief to sleep in his parents' bed.

It was a gigantic water bed. This was the sort of trap that was in fashion twenty years ago. The lack of comfort on offer was truly prodigious.

"Interesting," I observed. "You have to plan every move very carefully."

"It's like being in the canoe in the film *Deliverance.*"

"Exactly. Deliverance is getting out of the thing."

Rinri, who had planned a series of exceptional meals, shut himself away in the kitchen. I wandered around the concrete château.

Why could I not rid myself of the conviction that I was being watched by a camera—the impression that an invisible eye was following me. I made faces at the ceiling, then the walls: nothing happened. The enemy was cunning, pretending not to notice my misbehavior. Watch out.

Rinri came upon me sticking my tongue out at a piece of contemporary artwork.

"You don't like Nakagami's work?" he asked.

"I do, it's magnificent," I said enthusiastically to the canvas that was sublime with obscurity.

Rinri must have concluded that Belgians show their tongue to those paintings that truly move them.

Refined dishes awaited me on the table: sesame spinach, a chaudfroid of quails' eggs with chiso, and sea urchins. I did well by the meal, but I noticed that Rinri wasn't eating a thing.

"Well?"

"I don't like these dishes."

"Why did you make them?"

"For you. I like to watch you eat."

"I also like to watch you eat," I said, folding my arms in front of me.

"Please, eat some more, it's so beautiful."

"I'm on hunger strike until you bring your food to the table."

I was in torment, not only for fear of hurting him, but above all because I had to restrain myself from devouring these culinary marvels upon which my eyes were riveted.

Contrite, Rinri went to the kitchen and returned with some Italian-American salami and a jar of mayonnaise. I thought, "No, he can't possibly." And yet he did: he ate each slice of salami with a centimeter of mayonnaise on top. Vengeance or provocation? I feigned indifference and continued to indulge in my treasures of refinement, while he gushed with delight as he devoured his nightmarish repast. He intercepted my petrified expression and asked, sneering, "Didn't you want me to eat?"

"I'm enchanted," I lied. "We are each eating what we like best, that's great."

"I'd like to invite all my friends, to introduce them to you. Would you like that?"

I accepted. The party was set for five days hence.

It was vacation time. I did not set foot outside the concrete château. Rinri was treating me like a princess. In the living room, beneath Nakagami's painting, he had set up a lacquer writing desk for me. I had never had the opportunity to scribble in such conditions; they did not really suit me. There's nothing like bargain or even scrap material for stimulating the creative juices. The lacquer stuck to my fingers and I stained my manuscript.

Rinri looked at me in a stupor, and my pen stopped moving. Then, with a pleading air, he mimed the gesture of writing, and I understood that all I had to do was scribble anything at all for him to look contented. Like the hero in *The Shining*, I wrote over and over that I was going crazy. But there were no axes nearby to allow me to proceed to the next step of my emulation.

Until now, the only sort of life as part of a twosome I had ever experienced was with my sister. But she was so much my double that it was not life as a couple we shared, but rather an existence free from the quest for a perfect partner.

What I was experiencing with Rinri was something new, founded on a shared, and charming, awkwardness. Our life as a couple resembled the water-filled mattress we slept on: outmoded, uncomfortable, and funny. Our bond consisted in sharing a moving sense of malaise.

Every time he told me I was beautiful, Rinri had to interrupt everything: no matter what I was doing, I must stay in the same position, which never failed to be somewhat strange. Then the young fellow would walk all around me, saying, "Oh!", clearly enthralled. I didn't get it. One day I walked into the kitchen, where he was busy doing something. I was tempted by a tomato, and sunk my teeth into it. He let out a cry, and I thought it must be one of those famous beauty poses, so I froze. He grabbed the tomato from me and said that the fruit would spoil my complexion. Coming from a salami-mayonnaise eater, this was a bit rich, so I grabbed the tomato back from him. He sighed something desperate about the fleeting nature of whiteness.

From time to time the phone rang. He answered in the Japanese style, that is, saying so little that it was suspicious. The conversations lasted a maximum of ten seconds. I was not yet familiar with this Japanese custom and mused again that he must belong to the Yakuza, just as his white Mercedes had led me to believe. He would drive off in the car to go shopping and come back two hours later with three ginger roots. These purchases surely concealed some nefarious activities. After all, thanks to his sister, he must have ties with the Californian underworld.

Later, when his innocence was beyond any doubt, I would learn that the truth was far more incredible: he really did take two hours to choose three ginger roots.

Time hardly passed. I was free to go out, but I would not dream of it. Our hieratic sojourn fascinated me. Whenever Rinri left on his mysterious expeditions, I would have liked to make the most of my solitude in order to commit some evil deed: I would wander around the concrete château, looking for a chance to do some harm, but found nothing. Tired of trying, I sat down to write.

He came back. I greeted him ceremoniously by calling him *Danasama*—Excellency, my master. He pleaded his inferiority, bowed low before me, and called himself "your slave." Following these antics, he showed me what he had brought.

"Three ginger roots, magnificent!" I cried, ecstatic.

I already imagined myself taking part in a symposium on the wives of big-time criminals. "How did you find out that your fiancé was a crook?"

I tried to break the code of his behavior. Sometimes it was especially odd. He once placed a vast bamboo tub filled with sand in the middle of the living room. He smoothed the surface and then, standing over it, traced cabalistic signs in the sand with his bare foot.

I tried to decipher what he could be writing but, overcome with modesty, he erased it with his heel. This seemed to confirm my organized crime thesis. A picture of innocence, I then asked him the purpose of all this calligraphy.

"It helps me concentrate," he said.

"Concentrate on what?"

"Nothing. It's a good thing to be able to concentrate."

It didn't seem to be working: he forever had his head in the clouds. This began to remind me of someone.

"Christ, in the episode with the adulterous woman, draws signs in the earth with his foot," I said.

"Ah," he remarked, with the profound indifference any religious conversation inspired in him (with the exception of the Knights Templar; go figure).

"Did you know that the Romans on the cross, above Jesus's head, wrote the letters INRI? One more letter and it would spell your name."

I explained the acronym to him, and I managed to arouse his interest.

"Why do I have one letter more?" he asked.

"Perhaps because you are not Christ," I suggested.

"Or perhaps Christ had an additional initial. The R in the beginning might stand for ronin."

"Do you know many expressions where Japanese is mixed with Latin?" I asked, with a touch of irony.

"If Christ came back today, he wouldn't speak just one language."

"Yes, but he wouldn't speak Latin either."

"Why not? He would mix the various eras."

"And you think he would be a ronin?"

"Completely. Above all when he is crucified and he says, 'Why have you abandoned me?' A sentence worthy of a samurai who knows no master."

"You know your stuff. Have you read the Bible?"

"No. It was in *How to Become a Knight Templar*."

The title made me think I had arrived just in time.

"There's a book in Japanese with that title?"

"Yes. You've opened my eyes. I am the Jesus samurai."

"And how are you like Christ?"

"We'll see. I'm only twenty-one."

I was delighted with his conclusion, since it left him free to do as he liked.

The time came for the dinner with Rinri's friends. By morning, he was already apologizing for having to leave me behind and went to exile himself in the kitchen.

Apart from Hara and Masa, I had no idea whom I would meet. The two aforementioned fellows had nothing of the Yakuza about them, but then neither did Rinri. Perhaps his other friends would look the part.

I meditated for a long while in front of the vast painting by Nakagami. Even the faintest music would have disturbed me in my contemplation of this obscure splendor.

At around six o'clock, I saw Rinri emerge soaked in sweat from his pots and pans to align the place settings on a long table. I offered to help, but he would not let me. Then he rushed off to take a shower and came to join me. At six fifty-five he announced the arrival of the guests.

"Did you hear them arrive?" I asked.

"No. I invited them for seven fifteen. That means they'll be here at seven."

At seven o'clock sharp, the sound of a synthetic gong confirmed their punctuality. Eleven boys stood waiting outside the door, though they had not all arrived together.

Rinri showed them in, greeted them briefly, then disappeared into the kitchen. Hara and Masa gratified me with a nod. The nine others introduced themselves. The living room was just big enough to hold us all. I served the beer that Rinri had poured.

Everyone was looking at me in silence. I tried to stimulate conversation with the two boys I already knew—in vain; I turned to those I did not yet know—waste of time. Mentally I pleaded with Rinri to call us to dinner so that his presence might relieve this awkwardness. But apparently he had not finished preparing things yet.

The silence was so burdensome that I began a monologue on the first thing I could think of.

"I would never have suspected that the Japanese would be so fond of beer. But tonight I can see proof of what I've noticed so many times already: when you're offered a drink, you always choose beer."

They listened politely and didn't say thing.

"Were the Japanese already beer drinkers in the past?"

"I don't know," said Hara.

The others shook their heads to confirm their ignorance. Silence settled once again.

"In Belgium, we drink a lot of beer, too."

I was hoping that Hasa and Masa would remember the present I had brought on our previous evening together and would mention it, but no. I saw I must speak again and I told them everything I knew about the beer in my country. The eleven boys were behaving as if they had been invited to a lecture, listening respectfully; I dreaded that one of them might take out a notebook. To say I felt ridiculous is an understatement.

The moment I fell silent, it started all over. The eleven young men seemed to find the silence quite awkward; not one of them, however, was prepared to sacrifice himself to come to my assistance. At times I experimented with their attitude, pushing them to the very verge of their silence; five minutes, by the watch, went by, without a word. When we could bear the torture no longer, I set off again as best I could.

"Then there's Rodenbach, it's a red beer. It's called a wine-beer."

They immediately breathed more easily. I ended up hoping that they would treat me like a true speaker and start the Q & A.

When Rinri called to us to join him at the table, I sighed with relief. We were seated in an oblong fashion, I was in the middle, and then I noticed that there was no room for the master of the house.

"You forgot to set a plate for yourself," I murmured.

"No."

He went off to the kitchen again straight away and I couldn't question him further. He returned bearing a tray filled with marvels that he set down before us: dandelion fritters, chiso leaves stuffed with lotus root, slow-cooked broad beans with citron, deep-fried dwarf crabs to be crunched whole. After he had poured each of us some lukewarm saké, he disappeared and closed the kitchen door behind him.

That is when I understood: I would be the only host at the dinner. Rinri, like a true Japanese spouse, would remain cloistered in the place reserved for the slaves.

Visibly, I was the only one who seemed surprised by this state of affairs, unless the guests' politeness prevented them from showing their surprise. An approving murmur greeted the refinement of each dish. I was hoping that at the very least this delicious fare would loosen their tongues. Not a chance. Every dish was savored in religious silence.

I approved of their attitude. I've always found the obligation to speak while delighting in gastronomic wonders somewhat revolting. I concluded that Rinri had saved me after all, and devoted all my attention to licking my chops in contemplative silence.

Following this culinary ecstasy, I noticed that the guests were looking at me with a somewhat embarrassed and questioning gaze: they did not seem to understand why I was no longer looking after them. I decided to go on a speech strike. If they wanted to talk, then let them talk! After my lecture on Belgian beer, I felt entitled to my repose and my repast. I had removed my oratory apron.

Rinri came out to collect the empty dishes and brought each of us a lacquered bowl of orchid broth. I congratulated him fervently on his triumph. The others had accepted his role as Japanese spouse to such a degree that they ventured no more than a word or two of praise. With modesty the slave lowered his gaze and hurried back to his oubliette without saying a word.

The orchid broth was as lovely to look at it was insipid to taste. After we had gazed upon it for a while, there was nothing more to do. The silence became oppressive, once again.

It was then that Hara came out with the most incredible thing.

"You were telling us about the beer-wine."

My spoon stopped mid-flight and I understood: I was being told to continue my lecture. More precisely, it had been decreed that I would be the conversationalist for the evening.

The Japanese have invented an extraordinary profession: maker of conversations. They have noticed that the fastidious requirement of speech is the bane of dinner parties. In the Middle Ages, when there were imperial banquets, everyone remained silent and that was all to the good. In the nineteenth century the discovery of Western customs incited distinguished people to speak during meals. They discovered forthwith the tedium such effort entails, and for a time they assigned it to the geishas. These geishas rather quickly became increasingly rare, and Japanese ingenuity found a solution by creating the profession of conversationalist.

The conversationalist, before each mission, receives a file containing the seating arrangement and the identity of the guests. He (or she) must learn all he can about each guest, within the limits of propriety. During the meal the conversationalist, microphone in hand, moves around the banquet table and says, "*Mr. Toshiba here, president of the well-known corporation, would probably say to Mr. Sato, who graduated with him from the same high school, that he has not changed a great deal since that time. Mr. Sato would reply that the intensive practice of golf has helped him to keep in shape, as he said as recently as last month in the* Asahi Shimbun. *And Mr. Horie would suggest that in future he grant his interviews instead to* Mainichi Shimbun, *where Mr. Horie is in the position of editor-in-chief . . .*"

All this blah-blah, certainly not very interesting, but no worse than what you hear at dinners in the West, does have the uncontestable advantage of allowing the guests to eat in peace without feeling forced to speak. What is most astonishing is that they actually listen to the conversationalist.

"In Brussels they still make an artisanal Gueuze . . ." I said.

And off I went again. Rinri's friends immediately showed signs of contentment. The fact that there had been a pause made my disquisitions on the spontaneous fermentation of barley caused by natural yeasts all the more fascinating. Deep down I regretted I was not a union member; here I was an unpaid conversationalist, and to add insult to injury I had received no briefing about these people, so how could anyone expect me to exercise my profession under such conditions?

And yet exercise it I did, with bravery, thinking all the while about how I would get even with Rinri. He was taking the *catelya* broth bowls from the table and replacing them—to my utter frustration—with individual ramekins of *chawan mushi*, and here I was, prepared to sell my father and mother for a taste of this flan made with seafood and black mushrooms in fish fumet, which has to be eaten piping hot, knowing I wouldn't be able to swallow a single bite, because I was in the middle of explaining why Orval is the only Trappist beer that can be drunk at room temperature.

This was a Belgian version of the Last Supper, where a Christ from the Plat Pays brandishes a chalice filled not with wine but with beer, and saying, "This is my blood, the white beer of the new and eternal alliance, poured for you and for the multitudes in remission of sins, you shall do this in remembrance of my sacrifice, because while you are feasting on your scallops, some of us are working damn hard; and as for the thirteenth apostle who's hiding behind his hot stove and dares not even give me his Judas kiss, he'll get what's coming to him."

That individual—who actually dared to call himself the Jesus Samurai—was busy bringing out the dessert, whereof I saw nary a trace, from the blancmange to the ceremony tea, for I had reached my peroration:

"Many of the beers I've been talking about tonight can be bought at Kinokunya and some of them are even available at the Azabu supermarket."

I had earned myself something better than thundering applause: I noticed that they were all finishing their meal in perfect mental comfort, lulled by the background noise that my lecture had granted them. They had attained the repletion of the senses afforded by a banquet consumed in the utmost tranquility. I had not labored in vain.

After that, Rinri asked us to go into the living room, and joined us for coffee. The moment he was in our midst the guests once again became young men of twenty-one who had come to spend the evening at their friend's place: they began to converse as naturally as could be, to laugh, to listen while smoking to Freddy Mercury, to sprawl on the floor with their legs widespread. As for me, who had had to weather the silence of eleven bonzes and their flawless rigidity, I was overcome with despair.

I collapsed onto a sofa, as wasted as if I had drunk every one of the beers I'd mentioned that night, and I would not utter a single sound until all the invaders had left. I felt like strangling Rinri: all it would have taken was for him to honor us with his presence for three hours to spare me such an ordeal! How was I to keep from assassinating him?

When the intruders had taken their leave, I took a deep breath in order to stay calm.

"Why did you leave me alone with them for three hours?"

"So that you could get acquainted."

"You could have explained the operating instructions. No matter how I tried, they didn't say a word."

"They found you very entertaining. I'm very pleased: my friends like you and the party was a huge success."

Disheartened, I said nothing.

The boy must have understood for eventually he said, "They've forecast a typhoon for the weekend. It's Friday evening, my parents will be back on Monday. If you want, I'll close the shutters and not open them again until Monday. I'll barricade the door. No one can come in, and no one can get out."

I liked the idea. Rinri raised the drawbridge and pushed the button to lower the blinds. The outside world ceased to exist.

Three days later, reality forced its return. I opened the windows and stared, my eyes wide.

"Rinri, come see."

The garden had been devastated. The neighbors' tree had fallen on the roof of their house, dislodging tiles. A fissure split the earth.

"It's as if Godzilla came to visit," I said.

"I think the typhoon was stronger than they predicted. There must have been an earthquake."

I looked at him, repressing my desire to laugh. He gave a quick, sober smile. I liked the fact he was not at all boastful.

"I'll go clear away the traces of our passage in my parents' room," was all he said.

"I'll help you."

"No, go get dressed. They'll be here in fifteen minutes."

While he was cleaning the Augean stables, I put on my lightest dress: the heat was stifling.

Remarkably efficient, Rinri restored the premises to their original aspect in record time, and stood next to me to greet his family.

We were uttering the customary words and bowing when the grandparents and the mother pointed at me and began howling with laughter. Mortified, I inspected my person from head to foot, wondering what was so particular about me, but I found nothing.

The old people had come over to me and were touching the skin on my legs and shouting, "*Shiiroi ashi! Shiiroi ashi!*"

"Yes, my legs are white," I muttered.

Rinri's mother smiled and sneered, "In Japan, when a girl wears a short dress, she also wears panty hose, particularly when her legs are that white."

"Panty hose, in weather like this?" I exclaimed.

"Yes, in weather like this," she replied stiffly.

The father politely changed the subject by looking out at the garden.

"I expected the damage to be worse. The typhoon killed dozens of people on the coast. In Nagoya we didn't feel a thing. And you?"

"Nothing," said Rinri.

"Well, you're used to it. But what about you, Amélie, weren't you afraid?"

"No."

"You're a brave girl."

While the family took repossession of their domain, Rinri drove me home. The farther we drove from the concrete château, the more I felt I was returning to the real world. For seven days I had lived cut off from the sounds of the city, with no other view than a tiny Zen garden and a crepuscular painting by Nakagami. I had been treated as few princesses are treated. In comparison, Tokyo seemed familiar.

The typhoon and earthquake had left no perceptible traces. These were everyday occurrences.

The vacation was over. I went back to my Japanese class.

S eptember sacrificed me to the mosquitoes. They must have liked my blood: they were all over me. Rinri noticed the phenomenon and assured me I was the best protection against this plague of Egypt: my presence acted as a lightning rod.

No matter how much citronella or disgusting ointment I smeared on my skin, my fatal attraction prevailed. I recall insane evenings where, in addition to the sweltering heat, I had to endure innumerable bites. Camphorated alcohol provided little relief. Very quickly I discovered the only strategy: acceptance. Allow my body to itch and, above all, never scratch.

By dint of tolerating the intolerable, I began to find the sensation gratifying: once I accepted the itching it eventually lifted my soul and inoculated me with a valiant joy.

In Japan they burn *katorisenko* to keep the mosquitoes away. I never found out what those little green spirals are made of, but their slow burn drives the parasites away. I also resorted to them, if for no other reason than the pretty aspect of such strange incense, but my powers of seduction were so great that the mosquitoes could hardly be dissuaded by such a trifle. I received the tremendous proof of love from this buzzing tribe with a resignation which, once the ordeal had passed, was transformed into grace. My blood tickled with pleasure: deep within anything that throbs with pain there is sensual delight.

By virtue of this experience, I understood the purpose of the mosquito temples I had seen in India ten years earlier: the walls contained niches where the faithful offered their backs to a thousand bites at once. I had always wondered how the mosquitoes could feast in a promiscuity that far surpassed that of any orgy, and also how anyone could worship these winged divinities to the point of such extreme self-sacrifice. Most fascinating of all was imagining the swollen backs of those who partook in this insect bacchanalia.

Naturally, I would never have gone so far as to deliberately court such martyrdom. All the same, I was discovering that I could resign myself to it in a way that filled me with enthusiasm. The word "itching" had finally found its true justification: itching had translated into craving, and I had given up, I was *craven*, I offered myself to a banquet of winged lustful bugs; I was, through no choice of my own, a fully consenting feast.

My stoicism was strengthened by my trials: to refrain from scratching is a great education for the soul. And yet it was not without risk. One night the mosquitoes' poison so intoxicated my brain that for no reason at two o'clock in the morning I found myself stark naked outside my house. Miraculously the little street was deserted and no one saw me. I returned to my lodgings the instant I regained consciousness. To be the mistress of a thousand Japanese insects is not without repercussions.

In October the heat waned. Autumn began with its abusive splendor. When people ask me which is the best season to visit Japan, I always reply, October. There is sure to be a perfect balance of esthetics and climate.

The Japanese maple far surpasses the Canadian one for its beauty. Whenever he wanted to compliment me on my hands, Rinri would use the traditional expression, "Your hands are as perfect as the maple leaf."

"In which season?" I would ask, wondering whether I preferred my hands green, yellow, or red.

He invited me to visit his university, which was not the least bit prestigious, but whose gardens were worth a visit. I wore a long black velvet dress: I desperately wanted to emulate the ravishing Japanese students I would undoubtedly encounter on campus.

"You look like you're going to a ball," said Rinri.

In addition to eleven renowned universities, Japan boasts a thousand establishments that are so very easy that they are known as "train-station universities," equal in number to the country's train stations—no small thing in this land of railroads. I was being given the opportunity to explore the one where Rinri was spending a few years on vacation.

It was a luxurious colony where idle young people strolled. So bizarre were the outfits the girls wore that I was invisible. The place gave off the gentle atmosphere of a sanatorium.

From the age of three to the age of eighteen, the Japanese study as though possessed. From the age of twenty-five until they retire, they work like maniacs. From the age of eighteen to the age of twenty-five, they are only too aware that they have been granted a unique interval: this is their chance to blossom. Even those who have passed the formidable entrance exam to one of the eleven serious universities can breathe for a while: only the initial selection process is truly important. All the more reason for those attending a train-station university to sit back and relax.

Rinri sat down on a low wall and perched next to me.

"Look, what a fine view from the elevated railway. This is where I come to look at it and daydream."

I admired the view politely and said, "Do you sometimes go to class?"

"Yes. We'll be going."

"What sort of class?"

"Mmmmm. Hard to say."

He led me into a well-lit classroom, full of dozy students.

"Civilization class," he eventually told me.

"Which civilization?"

Deep reflection.

"American."

"I thought you were studying French."

"I am. American civilization is interesting."

I understood that our discussion defied any logic.

A middle-aged professor came in and took his place at the podium. If I try to recall what his presentation was about, this is all that comes to me: he talked about this and that. The students listened to him and did not move. My presence seemed to bother the instructor, and at the end of the class he came up to me and said, "I don't speak English."

"I'm Belgian," I replied.

This did not seem to reassure him. Belgium, for him, must have sounded like one of those obscure American states no one ever talks about, like Maryland. I could only be in his class for one purpose, to check on his information: hence his distrust.

"That was interesting," said Rinri, after the indeterminate class.

"Do you have another class now?"

"No," he replied, as if horrified by the suggestion he could actually do more work.

I commented on the fact that he had no friends among his fellow students at the university.

"I don't really see them often enough," he said.

He walked me around the lovely campus, and showed me all the places which afforded an unrestricted view of the elevated railway.

This glimpse into his studies made his schedule seem more nebulous than ever. From being fishy, it was now downright suspicious.

In the evening, when I asked him what he had done during the day, he replied that he had been very busy. Impossible to find out what had kept him so busy. What was most extraordinary was that he himself didn't even seem to know.

Once I was no longer full of paranoia, I understood that the years of university were the only ones during which the Japanese can allow themselves the exquisite luxury of frittering away their days. Their lives as schoolchildren, including leisure time, follow a strict schedule; their lives as working adults follow another schedule that is stricter still; therefore, the oasis of their student years is carefully devoted to something vague and indeterminate, if not a delectable nothing-at-all.

Rinri and I have a favorite film: *Tampopo,* by the director Juzo Itami. It relates the adventures of a young widow who searches the dregs of Japanese society for the recipe for the best noodle soup. It is a supreme parody, one of the funniest and most delightful films there is.

We watched it together many times, and often tried to re-enact certain scenes.

Going to the cinema in Tokyo was a disconcerting event. At first glance it did not seem to differ from the same experience in America or Europe. People sat themselves down in comfortable theaters, the show would begin with few commercials or announcements, some people would go quickly to the restroom and leave their wallet on their seat, for everyone to see. I suppose that when they came back not a yen was missing.

Nor was there any prudishness in the choice of films, and the coarsest things were projected without warning or rating: the Japanese are not puritanical. But whenever a woman came naked onto the screen, her fleece was blurred by a cloud: sex was not a problem, but clearly hairiness was off-putting.

Audience reactions were often astonishing. *Ben Hur* was playing: my passion for films about antiquity was compounded by my curiosity to see one in Tokyo. I invited Rinri. The dialogues between Ben Hur and Messala, subtitled in Japanese, were delightful—on reflection, they were no more absurd in Japanese than in English. One of the scenes shows the birth of Christ, with the divine light in the sky calling the wise men.

Behind me, I could hear a family exclaiming in wonder, "UFOs! UFOs!" Evidently, they were not the least bit perturbed by an invasion of flying saucers at the dawn of the Judeo-Christian era.

Rinri took me to see an old war film, *Tora Tora Tora*. It was showing in a little theater outside the center of town, and the audience were not the usual sort. Still, during the famous scene where the Japanese army bombs Pearl Harbor, most of the spectators applauded. I asked Rinri why he wanted me to see this film.

"It is one of the most poetic fictional films that I know," he replied, as serious as could be.

I didn't insist. This young man still had the capacity to leave me unhinged.

In November, the film *Dangerous Liaisons* by the English director Stephen Frears arrived in theaters in Tokyo. This adaptation of one of my favorite novels by one of my favorite filmmakers was bound to capture my interest. Rinri had not read the book and had no idea what it was about. On opening night the theater was packed. I had often observed Tokyo audiences writhing with laughter during violent films, but here they sat transfixed with horror by the Marquise de Merteuil. As for me, from start to finish I was in such a state of exultation that I could scarcely restrain my cries of ecstasy. It was just too good.

As we were leaving the theater and I was brimming over with enthusiasm, I noticed that Rinri was crying. I gave him a questioning look.

"That poor woman . . . That poor woman," he said over and over, sobbing.

"Which one?"

"The nice one."

And I understood what was going on: throughout the film, Rinri had identified with Madame de Tourvel. I did not dare ask him why: I was too afraid of what his reply might be. I tried to extricate him from his extravagant incarnation.

"Don't get so involved. The film isn't about you. Don't you think it was incredibly beautiful? The quality of the images and that incredible actor playing the lead role . . ."

My words were about as useful as urinating in a shamisen. For a full hour Rinri could do little else than repeat, over and over, between streams of tears, "That poor woman . . ."

I had never seen him like this, nor would I ever see him like this again. "At least he's not indifferent," I said to myself.

One weekend in mid-December I went off by myself to the mountains. Rinri had understood that this was one domain where it was pointless to try to accompany me, for I would be utterly inaccessible. I had not been anywhere without him for a long time, and the prospect was pleasing. Above all I was eager to discover the Japanese mountains in the snow.

I got off the train an hour and a half from Tokyo, at a village at the end of a valley which was the starting point for the ascent of the not-so-famous Kumotori Yama, a mountain of less than two thousand meters, which seemed reasonable to me for a first outing alone in the snow. According to the map, the hike should be quite comfortable, and it would offer an unrestricted view of Mount Fuji, my new friend.

My other criterion of choice was the name: Kumotori Yama means "the mountain of the cloud and the bird." The toponym already evoked an image, an engraving that I dreamt of exploring. The promiscuity of life in Tokyo easily gave birth to fantasies of being a hermit, and the mountains' lofty altitude provided the perfect safety valve.

One can never be reminded too often that Japan is a mountainous country. Two thirds of the land are practically uninhabited for that very reason. In Europe the mountains are busy and popular places, often serving as antechambers for cocktail parties, with innumerable snobbish resorts to show for it. In Japan, ski resorts are extremely rare, and there is no settled population living in the mountains, for it is a realm of death and witches. It is for this reason that the Empire retains a wildness that is often overlooked.

I had to overcome my fear of venturing into the mountains without an escort. When I was a child, my beloved Japanese governess would tell me stories about Yamamba, the nastiest of all the *onibaba* (witches), the one who reigns uncontested in the mountains, where she seizes upon solitary walkers to make them into a soup—solitary-walker soup, as Rousseauist a broth as can be—which has so haunted my imagination that I am convinced I know what it tastes like.

On the map I had located a hut not far from the summit, and I planned to spend the night there, unless Yamamba had already made plans to accommodate me in her cauldron.

I left the village and headed for the void. The path rose pleasantly through the snow, and I reveled in its virgin purity with all the giddy joy of a sultan. No one was walking ahead of me on this steep little Saturday morning climb. Until I reached a thousand meters, it was a charming stroll.

The forest of conifers and broad-leafed trees suddenly came to an end, unveiling a sky full of warnings I failed to heed. Before me lay one of the most beautiful landscapes in the world: on a long slope in the shape of a flared skirt was a snow-covered bamboo forest. The silence returned my ecstatic cries to me intact.

I have always felt a sort of boundless love for bamboo, a hybrid creature which the Japanese consider to be neither plant nor tree, which combines supple grace with the elegance of abundance. But I had never, as I recall, seen such bamboo as this, in the strange splendor of this snowy forest. Each slender tree struggled to bear its weight of snow and was crowned with whiteness, like very young girls burdened too soon with a sacred mission.

I walked through the forest as if I were entering another

world. Exaltation had replaced the notion of time, and I do not know how much time vanished into the ascent of the slope.

When I arrived at the forest's edge I saw the summit of Kumotori Yama, three hundred meters above me. It seemed very near, but not as near as the cloud heavy with snow that lolled on its left face. All that was missing, to justify the mountain's name, was the bird: I would be that feathered creature, careless of danger. I scurried swiftly toward the summit, which was easily accessible, and thought that nineteen hundred meters of altitude was for wimps, and that I would never underestimate myself in like manner ever again.

No sooner had I reached the peak than the cloud, acknowledging my avian nature, joined me there to fulfill the mountain's etymological destiny. The thick cloud was home to a blizzard, and all I could see was a giant swirl of snowflakes. I sat awestruck on the ground to watch the spectacle. I had climbed so quickly, I was steaming from the exertion and it felt exquisite to bare my head to this icy manna. I had never seen such a heavy snowfall: the snow was so thick and constant that I could scarcely keep my eyes open. "If you want to know the secret of snow, it is now that you must observe it: you are at the heart both of the factory and of the cannon." But industrial espionage was impossible: nothing is more mysterious than that which is unfolding before your eyes.

I do not know whether it was with me or with the mountain that the cloud had become besotted, but it did not move. I suddenly realized that my hair was as hoary as the ice beard on my chin: I must have looked like an old hermit.

"I'll go find shelter in the hut," I thought—and almost immediately I realized I hadn't seen any huts. Yet the map indicated one, slightly further down. The map dated from the previous year: could Yamamba have already destroyed the cabin in the meantime? I set off at once to look for it. The blizzard had completely covered the massif: I could not find my way out of the cloud. I spiraled around and down the peak, to be sure not to miss my goal. I could hardly see the tips of my outstretched fingers. There seemed to be no end to this waking sleep-walking.

My fingers struck something hard: the hut. "Saved!" I cried. I felt my way blindly around the little house, found the door, and stumbled inside.

There was nothing, no one there. The ground, the walls, and the ceiling were all made of wood. On the floor, an old blanket hid a *kotatsu:* my eyes opened wide at the sight of such comfort and I let out a cry of joy and wonder on discovering that the oven was burning hot. What luxury!

The *kotatsu* is more a way of life than a means of heating: in traditional homes, a square hole fills a vast space in the living room, and at the center of the hollow sits a metal stove. You sit on the floor with your legs dangling into the heat-filled pool, and the pit of torrid air is protected by a huge blanket.

I've known Japanese people who curse the *kotatsu:* "You spend all winter in prison under that pelisse, you're held captive in the hole and by the presence of others, and you're forced to submit to the pointless rambling of old people."

I had a *kotatsu* all to myself—all alone? Who was keeping the *kotatsu* going?

"Since the guard isn't here, take advantage of his absence to get undressed," I thought. I removed my clothes, which were soaked in sweat and snow, and hung them as best I could all around me so that they would dry. In my backpack I had pajamas, which I now put on, deriding myself: "Pajamas, and why not a ball gown while you're at it? It would have been more inspired of me to bring a change of clothes." Snug under the *kotatsu,* I ate some of my food supplies and listened to the groaning of the blizzard outside: I was jubilant.

I was also impatient for the master or mistress of the place to arrive: they must come by every day, no doubt, to fill the stove with fuel. I imagined the conversation I could have with this person, who was bound to be extraordinary.

Then, to my sudden dismay, I needed to pee. I should have thought of it earlier. The restroom was the mountain. If I went out into the blizzard in my pajamas I would lose my last dry things and I did not want to put my soaking clothes back on. There could be no two ways about it: I took off my pajamas, took a deep breath and ran outside as if I were jumping into the void. Barefoot in the snow, squatting there in the simplest of raiments, I did what I had to do in a mixture of horror and ecstasy. It was pitch dark and the whiteness of the swirling snow was invisible, could only be perceived by other senses: it felt white, tasted white, smelled white, sounded white. Dizzy with pain, I went back into the hut and dove under the *kotatsu*, relieved that the guard had not come upon me in such a pose. When the stove had dried my skin I put my pajamas back on.

I lay down under the blanket and tried to sleep. Gradually I realized that because of my gymnastic sprint into the outdoors, I could not get warm. No matter how I wrapped the blanket around me, no matter that I got as close as I dared to the stove, I was still freezing. The blizzard had bitten into me so deeply that I could not shake its glacial teeth from my body.

In the end I did something insane, but I had no choice: it was either a second- or third-degree burn and death: I chose the burn. I folded myself around the stove, right next to the scorching metal, with only my pajamas and a few blanket edges to protect me. That is when I realized how serious the problem was: I simply could not feel a thing. My skin had no perception of the very thing that should be toasting it.

And yet with my fingertips I was able to check that combustion was indeed occurring: only the pads of my fingers still had nerve endings. I was a corpse who had life in her fingertips and brain alone—a brain which had set off a futile alarm.

If only I could shiver! My body was so dead that it refused to comply with that life-saving reflex. It remained leaden with ice. Fortunately, it was suffering: I began to bless the pain which remained the ultimate proof that I still belonged to the world of the living. There is something suspicious about a martyrdom that reverses sensation: the stove's heat stung like cold. But that was far preferable to the terrible and imminent moment when I would no longer feel a thing.

And to think I had dreaded Yamamba's cauldron! My governess of bygone days had underestimated the mountain witch's cruelty. She did not transform solitary walkers into soup, but into frozen food—perhaps to be used in some future soup. The thought of it made me laugh and this first nervous reaction revived the others. At last I felt the salutary reflex: a shiver. My body began to vibrate like a machine.

Yet this did not ease my torment: knowing I would survive the night made it that much longer, and it seemed to last for ten years. I aged a century: riveted to the burning of a stove I could not feel, I spent the endless hours listening. Listening first of all, for hours, to the blizzard and its soft hammering against the mountainside; then the disquieting thickness of the silence the blizzard left behind.

And then I listened with the most animal hope in the world to the advent of the miracle known as morning—how slow it was in coming!

I had time to make this solemn vow to myself: "Whenever it shall be given to you to sleep in a bed, however humble, bless it and weep with joy!" To this day, I have never forsaken the solemnity of my oath.

While I lay listening for the first stirrings of dawn, I thought I heard footsteps in the hut. I did not have the courage to peek outside of the *kotatsu*, and was never able to verify whether these sounds came from an imagination overexcited by the cold, or an actual presence. I was so frightened that I trembled even more violently.

It was highly unlikely that it was an animal: the footsteps had a human sound. If someone was there, they must have been looking at my scattered clothes and they knew that I was under the *kotatsu*. I could have said something to indicate that I was not asleep, but I could not find the right words: fear had paralyzed my faculties.

The sound faded, a sound which may have never existed. Suddenly, holding my breath, I listened as the silence outside grew deeper: the sacred breath of the universe that heralds the dawn.

Hesitating no longer I sprung from the *kotatsu*: there was no one in the hut, nor was there the trace of anyone's passage. An unpleasant surprise awaited me: it was so cold inside the hut that my clothes had frozen. I thrust my feet into my trouser legs the way one carves a passage through the ice. The worst moment was the encounter between my frozen T-shirt and my back. Fortunately, I did not have time to stop and analyze these sensations. Departure was a matter of life or death: I had to rid myself of the chill which was eating away at me ever more voraciously.

How can I ever describe the shock that awaited me when I opened the door: I unsealed my tomb to discover the mystery. For a few moments I stood motionless before an unknown world that the blizzard had hidden from me the night before, then left buried deep beneath yards of a new whiteness. My ears had not been mistaken: dawn was stammering the first sounds of day. Not a puff of wind, not a single cry of a bird of prey, only glacial silence. No trace of footsteps in the snow: my nocturnal visitor, if she had existed, could be no one but Yamamba, come to check whether her trap for solitary walkers had functioned properly, and to gauge from the clothes hanging on the wall what sort of prey she had caught. I was deeply in her debt: without the *kotatsu*, I would not have survived. But if I wanted to continue to survive, I must wait no longer: it was ten past five in the morning.

I hurried off into the landscape. How wonderful to run! Space frees one from everything. There is not a single torment that can withstand the scattering of one's self into the universe. Why else would the world be so vast? Language is accurate: you run for your life. If you are dying, leave. If you are suffering, move. There is no other law, only movement.

Night had held me prisoner in Yamamba's realm; daylight set me free by restoring geography. I was jubilant: no, Yamamba, I do not have the soul of a bowl of soup, I am a living being and I am proving it to you, I'm out of here, you'll never know how bad I taste. My insomnia is as white as the snow around me, but I have the incredible energy of survivors and this mountain where I am running is too beautiful, I shall never consent to death on this mountainside. Each time I reach the peak of a slope, I discover a magnificent world, a world so virginal that I am frightened.

Yes, frightened. I have been running all this time, and I ought by now to have recognized the landscape I had seen the previous day. But this is not the case. Did the blizzard change the universe to such a degree? I grab my map and jab a finger at my reference point: Mount Fuji. It is far from here, but as soon as I see it I'll know I'm headed in the right direction. Unfortunately, it seems I have finally found the one place in Japan where you cannot see Mount Fuji: here, in this place where I am. I'll keep running, headed elsewhere.

I am lost. Being lost is intoxicating, makes me run all the faster. Yamamba, the joke's on you, no human being has ever come to this place. I feel boastful, to hide my terror. I escaped death during the night, but now it is trying to catch up with me. It has been written that I will depart this life at the age of twenty-two in the Japanese mountains. Will my corpse ever be found?

I don't want to die: I run. How can anyone run like this? Ten o'clock in the morning. The sky is an absolute blue, not the shadow of a cloud. It is a fine day for not dying. Zarathustra will save her skin. My legs are so long, they'll devour the peaks, you have no idea of their appetite.

I run but find nothing. Every time I arrive at the top of a slope, I pray that I shall see Mount Fuji, I call to it the way one calls to one's best friend, "Remember, old brother, I lay at the edge of your crater, I shouted to greet the sunrise, I'm family, wait for me at the top of the slope, I'll deny all other gods and believe in you alone, be there, I'm lost, all you need is to appear and I'll be saved, I'm at the top now, and you're not here!"

My energy has become the energy of despair, I keep running. It is nearly noon. For seven hours I have been lost, making things worse for myself. My motor is running on empty, night will fall and drown me in its black snow. This is the end of my little race on this earth. I don't want to believe it. Zarathustra cannot die, no one's ever seen such a thing.

Another slope. I'm losing faith, but climb all the same. I have nothing to lose, I'm already lost. My legs climb, they no longer even have the strength to be hungry. Every step costs a great deal. I've reached the ridge, no doubt it will be yet another disappointment. I run the last few meters.

Mount Fuji is there before me. I fall to my knees. No one knows how grand it is. I have found the place where you can see it in its entirety. I shout, I weep, how vast you are, you are calling me back to life! How beautiful you are!

Salvation strikes my guts, I pull my pants down, empty my bowels. Mount Fuji, I leave to you this undying testimony as proof that you are not dealing with just anybody, that I am not indifferent. I laugh with joy.

At noon on the dot. I look along the ridge, all I need to do now is follow it, my gaze reckons six hours' walking to reach the valley. That is nothing when you know you are going to survive.

I run along the ridge. For six hours of sunshine and blue sky, I shall have Mount Fuji all to myself. These six hours cannot suffice to contain my ecstasy. Exaltation is my fuel: there is nothing better. Never before has Zarathustra run so quickly and with such intoxication. I'm on familiar terms with Fuji now, I dance along the ridge. It is sublime, I would like for it to go on forever.

These six hours are the most beautiful in my life. I am marching my joy. I know why the music of triumph is called a march. Mount Fuji fills the sky, there's enough for everyone, but I have all of it to myself, those who are absent do not know what they're missing. No one knows as well as I do how grandiose and sublime Fuji is, which does not stop it from being the most pleasant of traveling companions. Fuji is my best friend. Zarathustra will deny herself nothing.

Here is the valley, in the dusk. The descent has gone by too quickly for me. I bow to my best friend and drop into the dale, and I can no longer see him. I already miss him. I scurry downhill at the speed of the fading light. I do not recognize the landscape at all. I must have been incredibly lost. I arrive in the village just as darkness falls.

A train takes me to Tokyo. Dazed, I look at the human beings around me. They do not seem shocked by my appearance. I conclude that my epic adventure is not visible on my face. At the station I take the metro. It is ten o'clock on a Sunday evening, the world is incredibly ordinary. But I, quite literally, do not yet have my feet on the ground.

I get out at my station. In my apartment there is heat, a bed, a bathtub: I'm as happy as a clam. The telephone is ringing off the hook. At the other end of the line, a human being is saying something.

"Who is this?" I say.

"What on earth, Amélie, it's me, Rinri. Don't you recognize my voice?"

I dare not tell him I had gone so far as to forget his very existence.

"You're back so late, I was getting worried."

"I'll tell you about it later. I'm too tired right now."

While the bathtub is filling, I look at myself in the mirror. From head to foot I am dark gray. Not a trace of any burn from the stove. The body is quite an invention. I step into the hot bath and suddenly my body spits out all the chill it had been keeping inside. I weep with despair and well-being. Survivors know that no one can ever understand them. In my case it is even worse: I have survived something too beautiful, too grand. I wish it were possible to share such a sublime thing with others, but I already know that I won't be able to explain it to them.

I lie down in my bed. I let out a shout: the bed is a trap. This much comfort is traumatizing. I think of the poor wretch wrapped around her stove: historically and geographically, I am only a stone's throw away from her. Henceforth, among the numerous other incarnations who inhabit me, there will be the poor wretch of the mountain. There will also be Zarathustra dancing with Mount Fuji on the ridge. I will always be those two souls, in addition to who I was before.

My various identities have not slept for a very long time, or perhaps they have never slept. I am devoured by a sleep that unites them within me.

What is terrible, after such an adventure, is that life goes on. The next day, in class, I felt like telling people about it. But the students couldn't have cared less. Their only concern was the upcoming vacation: just one more week and they'd be heading off to Hawaii.

The white Mercedes was waiting for me as I left the building.

"If you only knew what happened to me!"

"Shall we go for Chinese noodles? I'm starving."

Over my bowl, I tried desperately to evoke the snowy bamboo forest, the blizzard, the night in Yamamba's lair, the hours running lost on the mountain, my face to face encounter with Mount Fuji—and at this point Rinri burst out laughing, because I was spreading my arms as wide as I could to show him the size of the volcano. It is impossible to narrate the sublime. Either you're uninteresting, or you're comical.

Rinri took me by the hand.

"Will you spend Christmas with me?" he asked.

"All right."

"I'll take you on a trip from the twenty-third to the twenty-sixth."

"Where are we going?"

"You'll see. Bring warm clothes. No, we're not going to the mountains, I promise you."

"Does it mean anything to you, Christmas?"

"No. But there it will, yes, because I'll be with you."

Last week of classes. Soon I would no longer belong to the

student species. I had taken some tests, and at the beginning of the new year I would start work at one of the largest Japanese companies. My future was shaping up nicely.

A Canadian girl asked me if I was going to marry Rinri.

"I really don't know."

"Do be careful. These marriages produce the most awful children."

"What on earth are you talking about? Eurasians are magnificent."

"But dreadful. I have a girlfriend who married a Japanese guy. They have two children, six and four years old. They call their mother weewee and their father poop."

I burst out laughing.

"Maybe they have their reasons," I said.

"How can you laugh? And what if it happens to you?"

"I don't think I'll be having kids."

"Oh. Why? That's not normal."

I walked away humming a song by Georges Brassens in my head: "No, those good folk sure don't like it / When you head off down a different path . . ."

On the morning of December 23, the white Mercedes was waiting under a dark gray sky. The drive was long, ugly and depressing, because Japan can also be an ordinary country.

"I know I'll see, but where are we going?"

"Even if the landscape suggests otherwise, you won't be disappointed."

We've come such a long way since "Omreeeh!" I thought. Undoubtedly you can't make a good French speaker without breaking eggs.

Suddenly, the sea.

"The Sea of Japan," said Rinri ceremoniously.

"I first got to know it when I was little, in Tottori. I almost drowned."

"You are alive," concluded Rinri, to excuse the sacred sea. He parked the car in the port of Niigata.

"We're taking the boat to the island of Sado."

I jumped for joy. I had always dreamt of visiting this island famed for its beauty and wilderness. Rinri took a suitcase big as a steamer trunk from the car. The crossing seemed icy cold and endless.

"The Sea of Japan is a virile sea," said Rinri.

This was a remark I had already heard uttered countless times in Japan, and I had never commented on it, so greatly perplexed did it leave me. My primitive imagination searched the breaking waves for beard bristle.

The boat left us on the island, where the rudimentary port was a sharp contrast to the one in Niigata. A bus from the 1960s drove us to an old rambling inn half an hour away. This *ryokan* was located in the center of the island: you could hear the sea more than you could actually see it. All around was nothing but virtually virgin nature.

It began to snow. I was exultant, and suggested we go for a walk.

"Tomorrow," said Rinri. "It's four o'clock, but I'm exhausted from driving."

No doubt he wanted to enjoy the luxury of the inn, and I could not blame him for that. The magnificent traditional rooms were fragrant with fresh tatami, and each one had a vast Zen tub, continuously filled by a bamboo pipe spurting piping hot water. To keep it from spilling over, the tub's rough stone had a hole pierced in it, above which the ideogram representing a burning haystack signified nothingness.

"Metaphysics!" I cried.

After we had soaped ourselves and rinsed off, in keeping with the ritual, Rinri and I settled into the incredible bathtub with every intention of never leaving it.

"It seems there's an even more famous *furo* somewhere in the shared part of the hotel," he said.

"It can't be better than the one in our own bedroom," I replied.

"You're wrong. It's ten times bigger than this one and is fed by a network of bamboos, and it's under the open sky."

This last argument convinced me. I insisted we go there. There was no one around, fortunately, because in keeping with the ancient ritual, the sexes were not separated.

To be naked in a warm bath while snowflakes are falling: I uttered little cries of ecstasy. It was such a pleasure to be in this tub and feel the icy crystals land upon my head.

Half an hour later Rinri got out of the *furo* and put on his *yukata*.

"Already?" I asked, indignant.

"It's not good for your health to stay in too long. Come on out."

"Out of the question, I'm staying."

"Suit yourself. I'm going back to the room. Don't be long."

Delighted to be on my own, I did a dead man's float, so that my entire body could enjoy the miraculous encounter with the icy elements: how exquisite it was to be stoned with sorbet, and to feel my underside marinating in steaming water.

Alas, my solitude did not last: a little old man from the hotel's maintenance crew came to sweep around the edges of the bath. I folded my nakedness back into the water at once, and made swirling gestures with my hands and feet to clothe myself.

Small and spindly as a shrub, the eighty-year-old had probably never left the island. With his broom of twigs he conscientiously swept the edges of the tub. His implacable face was reassuring. But when he had gone all around, he started all over again. And didn't it seem fishy that he had waited for Rinri to leave before starting his task?

I noticed that the old man was brushing away the snowflakes the moment they landed around the edge of the *furo*. Now, it was going to snow for a long time: we had not yet seen the last of it. And truthfully I could not get out of the tub while he was there: between the moment when I would spring from the tub and the moment I could grab my *yukata*, there would be an instant when I would irremediably naked.

To be sure, I was in no great danger. With all his clothes on my little old islander must have weighed no more than ninety pounds, and his age made him even less dangerous. Yet the situation was no less unpleasant for all that. My arms and legs were getting tired. Their labors now left something to be desired and the opacity of the bath could no longer be guaranteed. Although he did not show it, great-grandfather must have found the spectacle highly interesting.

I decided it was time to deal with him. With my chin I pointed toward his broom and shouted harshly, "*Iranai!*"

Which, in everyday parlance means, "It's not necessary!"

He told me he did not speak English. Such a reply was proof of the fellow's lack of good faith, and I no longer had any doubts regarding the perverse nature of his presence.

I had not yet touched bottom, however: the worst came when I could feel in my body the warning signals of a fainting spell. Rinri was right, one should not stay too long in this steaming stew. I had not been aware of it until now, but my strength had been melting away. I could see the moment coming when I would well and truly pass out in the *furo,* and the old man, on the pretext that he was rescuing me, could do whatever he liked with me.

Help.

Moreover, the phase preceding a fainting spell is truly atrocious. As if ten million ants were invading the interior of your body, transforming your guts into nausea. Along with the invasion comes an indescribable weakness. Amélie, get out of there while you still can, in other words, right now. He'll see you naked, so what, things could get a lot worse.

The old sweeper watched as a white waterspout burst from the bath and threw itself onto the *yukata*, cloaked itself and scurried out of there at a run. I rushed blindly to the bedroom where Rinri saw me come hurtling in then collapse onto the futon. I recall that the moment I gave myself permission to pass out, some instinct made me look at the clock and I saw the time: 18:46. And then I slipped into a bottomless well.

I traveled. I explored the court at Kyoto in the seventeenth century. A procession of aristocrats of both sexes, sumptuously dressed in purple kimonos, bloomed upon the hillside. A woman came forward, her sleeves those of a lady-in-waiting, Lady Murasaki perhaps, and, accompanying herself on the koto, she began to sing an ode to the glory of the nights of Nagasaki, no doubt for the richness of the rhymes.

These activities lasted several decades. I had time to settle into this Japanese past, where I exercised the enviable profession of saké taster. Cupbearer in Kyoto was a position I had no intention of abandoning when I was brutally called back by December 23, 1989. The clock indicated 19:10. How could I have experienced all that in twenty-four minutes?

Rinri had respected my temporary fainting spell. Sitting next to me, he asked what had happened. I talked about the seventeenth century; he listened politely, then said, "Yes, but before that?"

The events came back to me, and in a less poetic tone I told him the story of the dirty old man who had come to ogle the Naked Whitewoman under the pretext of sweeping.

Rinri clapped his hands and burst out laughing, "I love that story! You have to tell it to me often."

I was disconcerted by his reaction. If I had been expecting some indignation on his part, I might as well have spared myself the trouble: Rinri was delighted, and he mimed the scene, bent over double like some old dodderer with his imaginary broom, glancing menacingly toward the baths; then he imitated me, gesticulating and saying "*Iranai,*" then he replied in a quavering voice that he didn't speak English, all frequently interspersed with peals of laughter. I interrupted him with a remark: "The island is well-named, you've turned sadistic."

He laughed all the harder. In Japanese the pun was perfect, for the name of the Divine Marquis is pronounced Sado.

There was a knock on the door.

"Are you ready for the banquet?" asked Rinri.

The panel slid open and two charming country girls brought in some low tables on which they proceeded to set out dish upon dish of delectable treats.

The *kaiseki* chased all thoughts of the horrid old man from my mind and I set out to do justice by it. Several different sakés were served: I concluded that my fainting dream had been a premonition and I waited curiously to see what would come next.

The next morning the island of Sado was white with snow.

Rinri took me to the northernmost shore.

"You see over there?" he said, pointing across the sea toward the horizon. "That's where Vladivostok is."

I admired his imagination. But he was right: the only land you could conceive of behind such imprisoning clouds was Siberia.

"Shall we walk around the island along the coast?" I suggested.

"You've no idea, that would take far too long."

"Oh come on, how often do you get to see the shoreline covered with snow?"

"In Japan, often enough."

After four hours of walking, with the wind coming from the sea, I gave up.

"Just as well," said Rinri. "To go all the way around, it

would take another ten hours, never mind getting back to the inn, which is in the middle of Sado."

"We'd better take the shortest route," I murmured through blue lips.

"In that case, we'll be back in our room in two hours."

The hinterland turned out to be infinitely more beautiful and entrancing than the coast. Best of all were the immense snowy persimmon orchards: by some strange fluke of nature, persimmon trees, which lose their leaves in winter like any other fruit tree, do not lose their fruit, even when they have grown beyond ripeness. In extreme cases, the living trees bear their dead fruit, evoking a deposition from the cross. But this wasn't the time to be thinking about dead bodies—the sight of the most extraordinary Christmas trees was offered to me: black, bare trees laden with persimmons as ripe as they come, with each bright orange fruit bearing a luminous snowy crown.

One tree alone adorned in this way would have been enough to exalt me. But I saw battalions of trees standing at attention in deserted meadows, and my head was spinning with admiration and desire, for I take great delight in ripe persimmons. Alas, no matter how high I jumped, I could not reach a single one.

"This is a fairy tale for one's eyes alone," I thought. "One mustn't always want to eat everything one sees." But my own reasoning failed to convince me.

"Let's go," said Rinri, "we'll freeze to death."

Back at the inn he left the room. I took a quick bath and collapsed on the futon. Sound asleep, I did not hear him come back in. When he woke me, it was seven in the evening. Shortly thereafter, the ladies brought us our banquet.

There was a culinary incident. They brought little live octopuses. I was familiar with the principle and I had already encountered this unpleasant experience: the idea was to eat the fish or the seafood the moment they were killed, there, before your eyes, in order to be sure they were absolutely fresh. I had lost count of how many filets of still-quivering sea bream I had tasted, while a delighted restaurateur looked on and said, "It's alive, isn't it? Can you feel the taste of life?" I never found that the taste merited such a barbarian custom.

When I saw the octopuses, I was sorrier still: first of all because there is nothing more charming than these little beasties with their tentacles, and secondly because I have never fancied raw octopus. But it would have been impolite to refuse a dish.

In the instant of the murder I looked away. One of the ladies placed the first victim on my plate. This tiny octopus, lovely as a tulip, broke my heart. "Chew quickly, swallow, and then tell them you're not hungry anymore," I instructed myself.

I shoved it into my mouth and tried to plant my teeth into it. Then the most dreadful thing happened: the octopus's nerves, still alive, commanded it to resist, and the vengeful corpse fastened onto my tongue with all its tentacles. And would not let go. I was screaming as loudly as you can scream when you have had your tongue swallowed whole by an octopus. I stuck it out to show them what had happened: the ladies burst out laughing. I tried to detach the beast with my fingers: impossible, the suction cups were firmly stuck. I pictured the instant when I would tear my own tongue out.

Horrified, Rinri looked at me without moving. At least I felt that someone understood me. I moaned through my nose in hopes that the ladies would stop laughing. One of them seemed to think that the joke had gone on long enough, so she came and poked a chopstick into a precise spot on my aggressor, who instantly let go. If it was that simple, why hadn't she come to the rescue sooner? I contemplated the octopus I had spit out onto my plate and thought that this island did indeed deserve its name.

When the ladies had cleared out, Rinri asked me if I had

recovered from my trauma. I replied with a laugh that this was an astonishing Christmas Eve.

"I have a present for you," he said.

And he brought me a bundle of jade green silk, weighted with some heavy objects.

"What's inside the *furoshiki?*"

"Open it."

I untied the traditional scarf, thinking all the while how lovely it was to offer gifts in this way, and let out a cry: the *furoshiki* was filled with persimmons that the winter had transformed into giant gemstones.

"How did you do this?"

"While you were asleep I went back to the orchard and climbed the trees."

I jumped up to hug him: and here I had been thinking he'd gone off on some mafia business!

"Can you eat some, please?"

I never understood why he was so fond of watching me eat, but I joyfully complied. To think that some people assassinate octopuses when there are ripe persimmons for the plucking! The pulp of the fruit, exalted by frost, had the flavor of a sorbet of precious gems. Snow possesses extraordinary gastronomic powers: it concentrates sapid juices and sharpens taste. It acts like a miraculously delicate form of cooking.

In seventh heaven, I tasted the persimmons one after the other, my eyes moist with pleasure. I did not stop until there were no munitions left. The scarf was empty.

Rinri was staring at me, gasping for breath. I asked him if he had enjoyed the performance. He lifted up the stained *furoshiki* and handed me a tiny gauze case that had been hidden underneath. I opened it with some trepidation, immediately justified: a platinum ring, inlaid with an amethyst.

"Your father has gone all out on this one," I stammered.

"Do you want to marry me?"

"Do you think I have a single finger left?" I replied, lifting my hands which were already laden with paternal masterworks.

Rinri went into a long arithmetic demonstration, explaining that if I moved the onyx to my little finger, the zircon to the middle, the white gold to my thumb and the opal to the index, I could free up a ring finger.

"Ingenious," I remarked.

"Right. You don't want to," he said.

"I didn't say that. We are so young."

"You don't want to," he repeated coldly.

"Before marriage, there is a period known as an engagement."

"Stop talking to me as if I were a Martian. I know what an engagement is."

"Don't you think it's a nice word?"

"You're talking about an engagement because it's a nice word or simply because you refuse to marry me?"

"I just want things to follow a certain order."

"Why?"

"I have principles," I heard myself say, flabbergasted.

The Japanese have great respect for this type of reasoning.

"How long does an engagement last?" asked Rinri, as if inquiring into the rules and regulations.

"There's no set time."

He did not seem to like this reply.

"Engagement contains the idea of a gage, a pledge," I added, to plead my cause. "The fiancée pledges her troth. It's lovely, don't you think? Whereas the meaning of the word marriage is filled with platitudes, just like the contract that defines it."

"So you don't ever want to marry me," concluded Rinri.

"I didn't say that," I said, aware that I had gone too far.

There was an awkward silence, which I finally broke. "I accept your engagement ring."

He performed the rotations he had suggested on my erstwhile very gothic fingers and slid the amethyst imprisoned in platinum onto the liberated ring finger.

"Do you know that the Ancients claimed that amethysts have the power to cure drunkenness?"

"I'm going to need it," said Rinri, once again very loving.

A few hours later he fell asleep and I began my insomnia. Whenever I thought of Rinri's proposal, I felt like I was reliving the moment when the tentacles of the dead octopus latched onto my tongue. This loathsome association of ideas was in no way owing to the near simultaneity of the two episodes. I tried to reassure myself by thinking that I had managed to free myself from the embrace of the suction cups, and to adjourn *sine die* the matrimonial danger.

And there had been the business with the persimmons. Eve in the garden had not managed to pick the desired fruit. The new Adam was acquainted with gallantry and went to pick her an entire shipload, and then, with great tenderness, watched her eat. The new Eve, made selfish through her sin, did not so much as offer him a nibble.

I was very fond of this remake: it seemed to me more civilized than the classic version. However, the end of the story became nebulous with that marriage proposal. Why must pleasure always have a price? And why must one always pay for sensual delight with the loss of original lightness?

After hours spent ruminating on this grave matter, I eventually fell into a fitful sleep. My dream was predictable: in a church, a priest was marrying me to a giant octopus. He was placing the ring on my finger and I was slipping a ring onto each tentacle. The man of God was saying, "You may now kiss the bride."

The octopus took my tongue into his oral cavity and would not let go.

The following morning, the provincial bus took us back to the ferry landing. On board, as we watched the island recede, Rinri said, "It's sad to leave Sado."

"Yes," I replied, only half-sincere.

I would miss the persimmons.

Rinri looked at me with a moist gaze and exclaimed, "My Sado fiancée!"

This looked promising.

At Niigata the Mercedes awaited for the drive back to Tokyo. During the trip I asked myself the burning question: why hadn't I said no? I did not want to marry Rinri. Besides, I had disliked the idea of marriage from time immemorial. That being the case, what had prevented me from refusing?

The explanation was that I did like Rinri. To refuse would have meant breaking up, something I did not want. So much friendship and laughter bound me to this sentimental young man. I was loath to give up his charming company.

I blessed whoever it was who had invented engagements. Life has its share of trials; a mechanism of fluids allows us, all the same, to make our way through them. The Bible—that superb treatise on morality for use by pebbles, rocks and standing stones, teaches us admirable petrified principles, "may Thy word be yes? Yes? No? No. What is added comes from the Devil"—and those who comply with the Bible are untouchable beings, all of a piece, esteemed by all. At the other extreme you have creatures who are incapable of any granitical behavior and who, to get by, can only worm their way, infiltrate, circumvent. When asked whether yes or no they would like to marry so-and-so, they propose an engagement, liquid nuptials. The stony patriarchs see such women as traitors or liars, although they are sincere, in the manner of water. If I am water, what is the point of my saying Yes, I shall marry you? That would be a lie. Water cannot be contained. Yes, I shall irrigate you, lavish you with my riches, refresh you, appease your thirst, but how can I know the course my river shall follow: you shall never bathe twice in the same fiancée.

These fluid beings draw the scorn of the crowd, although their undulating attitudes enable them to avoid so much conflict. The vast and virtuous blocks of stone, whose praises one never stops singing, are the ones who start wars. To be sure, with Rinri, it was not international politics that were at stake, but I did have to confront a choice between two enormous risks: one was Yes, synonymous with eternity, security, solidity, stability and other words that freeze water; the other was No, synonymous with wrenching separation and despair, and here-I-believed-you-loved-me-get-out-of-my-sight-yet-you-seemed-so-happy-when— and other definitive utterances that make water boil with indignation, for they are unfair, barbarian accusations.

Such a relief to have found the engagement solution! A liquid response, in that it resolved nothing and merely postponed the matter until later. But preserving time is life's great endeavor.

In Tokyo, as a precaution, I spoke to no one about the engagement.

At the beginning of January, 1990, I started work at one of the seven huge Japanese corporations which, under the guise of business, are the veritable holders of power in Japan. Like any ordinary employee, I thought I would be working there for forty years or more.

In my treatise on fear and trembling, I have related the reasons I found it difficult to stay to the end of my one-year contract.

It was a descent into a hell of the utmost banality. My lot did not differ greatly from that of the vast majority of Japanese employees, though it was made worse by my condition as a foreigner, and by a certain personal genius for awkward behavior.

In the evening I would meet up with Rinri and tell him about my day. Not a single one went by without its share of humiliation. Rinri listened, his suffering greater than what I had endured, and when I finished my story he would shake his head and ask my forgiveness in the name of his compatriots.

I assured him that it was not his compatriots who were in question. I had numerous precious allies within the company. When all is said and done, my martyrdom was the work of one person alone, as is often the case in the world of work. To be sure, she had support in influential quarters, but all that was needed was a change of attitude on her part for my fate to take a vastly different turn.

I was leading a double life. Slave by day, fiancée by night. I might have got something out of it if the nights had not been so short: I did not join Rinri until ten in the evening and I had already, at that time, begun to get up at four o'clock in the morning to write. Not to mention the occasional night I spent at the company, having failed to finish my assigned task.

Weekends disappeared into an abyss, leaving no trace in memory. I would get up late, put the dirty laundry into the machine, write for a while, then put the laundry out to dry. Thoroughly wrung out by these activities, I collapsed on the bed with all the week's weariness. Rinri, as always, wanted to take me out to do all sorts of things; I no longer had the strength. The most he was able to get out of me consisted of going to a movie on a Saturday evening. And there were times when I fell asleep.

Rinri bravely put up with his battered fiancée. I was the one who could no longer put up with her. At work, I understood who I was; I understood nothing about the zombie I became once I was away from the company.

On the metro, headed for my torture chamber, I would think back on my former life. Hardly any time at all separated my two lives. It was hard to believe. What, in this short space, had become of Zarathustra? Had I really climbed the Japanese mountains with my bare legs? Had I really danced with Mount Fuji as I remembered? And had I really had so much fun with this boy, who now sat watching me sleep?

If only I could have convinced myself that this was just a bad patch! But no, everything led me to believe that I was now fully cognizant of the common fate that would be mine for the next forty years. I confided in Rinri, who hastened to say, "Stop working. Marry me. It will put an end to your worries."

It was tempting. I could leave my torturer behind, enjoy material comfort, delight in doing nothing all the livelong day, and the only condition was to live side by side with a charming young man: who would have hesitated?

But—without being able to explain why—I was expecting something more. I did not know what it would consist of, but I knew that it was part of my hopes and dreams. The less you know about the nature of your desire, the more violent that desire becomes.

The conscious part of my dream was writing, which already took up a great deal of my time. To be sure, I did not fill myself with illusions to the point of believing I would be published someday, or still less of imagining that I might make a living at it. But I had an absurd determination to see what would come of it, if only to be sure I would never regret not having made the effort.

Before Japan, I'd never thought about writing seriously. Too strong was my dread of the humiliation I would no doubt undergo in the form of editorial rejection letters.

But now, given the tenor of my everyday life, there was no humiliation on earth that could still affect me.

Yet for all that, nothing was certain. The voice of reason screamed at me to accept the marriage: "Not only will you be rich without working, you will also have the best of husbands. You have never met a kinder, funnier, more interesting boy. He has nothing but good qualities. He loves you, and no doubt you love him more than you know. To refuse to marry Rinri is tantamount to committing suicide."

I could not bring myself to do it. The Yes would not come out of my mouth. As I had done on Sado Island, I sidestepped the issue by prevaricating.

The proposal was frequently reiterated. The reply was always evasive. Although it might not seem that way, I was dying of shame. I had the impression I was making everyone miserable, myself for starters.

Work was hell. Rinri showed me a tenderness I did not deserve. There were times I thought that my professional martyrdom was a just punishment for my amorous ingratitude. Japan took back from my waking hours what Rinri gave me at night. This story was going to end badly.

And there were times when I was relieved to go to work. When I preferred open warfare to an uneasy truce. And I preferred being an involuntary martyr to a willing torturer. I have always been horrified by power, but it is less painful for me to submit to it than to wield it.

The worst accidents in life are accidents of language. One weekday evening after midnight, just as sleep was pulling me to the bottom, Rinri asked for my hand in marriage for the two hundred and fortieth time. Too tired to be evasive, I answered no and fell asleep at once.

In the morning by my writing desk I found a note from the young man: "Thank you, I am very happy."

I drew conclusions of a high moral value: "You made someone happy by being clear. You have dared to say no. There is nothing kind about leaving someone with false hopes. Ambiguity is the source of pain, etc."

I went to work for my daily dose of humiliation. That evening, when I left work, Rinri was waiting for me.

"I'm taking you out to eat."

"Are you sure? I'm exhausted."

"It won't take long."

Over our bowls of mountain fern soup, Rinri told me that his parents were delighted with the excellent news. I burst out laughing and said, "I'm not surprised."

"Particularly my father."

"There you do surprise me. I would have thought it was your mother rather who'd be delighted."

"It's harder for a mother to see her son leave home."

This remark set off a faint alarm bell in my brain. I had no doubt that I had said No the night before, but I was no longer certain of the terms in which the matrimonial question had been couched. If Rinri had questioned me in the negative, which is common in this complicated country, I was done for. I tried to recall the Japanese grammar rules for replying to negative questions, which are as complex as trying to recall the steps to the tango. My exhausted brain could not find its way out, so I decided to try an experiment. I took hold of the saké carafe and said, "Do you not want any more saké?"

"No," replied the young man politely.

I put the useless carafe back on the table. Rinri seemed disconcerted but, as he did not want to order me about, he took the carafe and served himself.

I hid my face behind my hands. Now I understood. He must have asked, "Do you still not want to marry me?" And I had answered in the Western fashion. After midnight, I have the infelicitous flaw of turning into an Aristotelean.

It was awful. I knew myself well enough to realize that I would not have the strength to set the matter straight. I was incapable of being unpleasant to someone who was kind. I would sacrifice myself in order not to disappoint him.

I wondered whether Rinri had not asked the question in the negative on purpose. I couldn't believe it. But I did not doubt that his subconscious had dictated this Machiavellian plan.

Thus, by virtue of a linguistic misunderstanding, I was going to marry this charming boy, with his perverse subconscious. How could I ever find my way out of such a hornet's nest?

"I've informed your parents," he added. "They shrieked with delight."

Naturally. Rinri was the darling of my mother and father.

"Would it not have been better for me to let them know?" I asked, determined to ask nothing but negative questions henceforth.

Rinri sidestepped the pitfall.

"I know you are working and I am still a student. I thought you wouldn't have time. Are you cross with me?"

"No," I replied, so sorry he had not asked the question in a negative way, which would have allowed me, under the pretext of cultural differences, to tell him my thoughts.

I'm in up to here already, I concluded, so what difference will it make?

"What date would you prefer?" he asked.

That was all I needed.

"Let's not decide everything in such a short time," I replied.

"And in any case, as long as I am working for Yumimoto it will be impossible."

"I understand. When does your contract end?"

"Beginning of January."

Rinri finished his soup and declared, "1991, then. It's a palindrome year. A good year for getting married."

The year 1990 ended in utter confusion.

Only one thing was clear: I was resigning from my job. The Yumimoto company would soon have to do without my invaluable services.

I would have dearly liked to resign from my marriage as well. Unfortunately, Rinri was more disarmingly kind than ever.

One night, I heard an inner voice saying to me, "Remember the lesson of Kumotori Yama. When Yamamba was holding you prisoner, you found the solution: flight. You can't escape through words? Then escape with your feet."

When fleeing a country is the issue, one's feet take the form of an airplane: on the sly, I bought a ticket from Tokyo to Brussels. One way.

"The round trip is cheaper," said the saleswoman.

"A one way," I insisted.

Freedom is priceless.

This was that long-ago era before electronic tickets: the plane ticket—made of thick, laminated card stock—had a palpable reality at the bottom of my purse, or in my pocket, where my hand went to seek reassurance fifty times a day. The inconvenience was that if you lost it, obtaining a duplicate would be nothing short of miraculous. But there was no risk of me losing this symbol of my freedom.

As his family had gone to Nagoya, I spent the three days over New Year's with Rinri in the concrete château, the only three days in which it is truly forbidden to do any work. This even applies to cooking: his mother had filled traditional lacquer boxes with the cold dishes that custom had assigned to these three days of public holiday: buckwheat noodles, sweet beans, rice cakes and other oddities more pleasing to the eye than palate.

"Don't feel obliged to eat that stuff," said Rinri, who was shamelessly making himself spaghetti.

I did not feel obliged: it wasn't very good, but I was fascinated by the sheen on the sugary beans, reflected in the deep-black lacquer. I lifted them one by one with my chopsticks, keeping the square box level with my eyes in order not to miss a single scrap of the spectacle.

Thanks to the airline ticket hidden in my pocket, these were delightful days. I observed the young man with a kindly curiosity: so this was the boy I had been happy with for two whole years and whom I was about to run away from. What a strange story, what an absurd waste—did he not have the most beautiful nape imaginable, the most exquisite manners, had I not found the closest thing to an ideal shared life in his company? For I felt good around him, curious and comfortable at the same time.

And did he not belong to this country I loved more than any other? Was he not the only proof that the adored island was not rejecting me? Was he not offering me the simplest and most legal way to acquire the fabulous nationality?

Finally, were my feelings for him not sincere? Of course they were. I liked him very much and this very much, for me, was something new. And yet the need to use an adverbial phrase to qualify my feelings convinced me of the urgency of departure.

If even for an instant I imagined destroying my airplane ticket, my tender friendship for Rinri turned into hostile dread. All it took, on the other hand, was one touch of its shiny surface to feel a rush of jubilation and guilt that resembled love but was not love—like sacred music that contaminates the soul with an élan that resembles faith but is not faith.

Sometimes he took me into his arms without saying a thing. I would not want my worst enemy to feel what I felt then. And at no time did Rinri ever behave in a vile or vulgar or petty manner. If he had, it might have made things easier for me.

"Basically, there is not an evil bone in your body," I told him.

He said nothing, astonished, and eventually asked me if this was a question. That seemed to me an edifying reply.

I'd hit the nail on the head: it was because there was nothing evil in him that I liked him so very much. And yet, it was because he was a stranger to evil that I had no love for him. It is not that I have any affinity for evil. But no dish is sublime unless it contains a touch of vinegar. Beethoven's Ninth would be unbearable to listen to if it did not have moments of desperate hesitation. Jesus would not have inspired so many men had he not, at times, uttered words that were so close to hatred.

One thought led to another: "Are you still the Jesus samurai?"

Rinri replied with extraordinary ingenuity, "Oh, yes. I'd forgotten all about it."

"Well, are you or aren't you?"

"Yes," he said, as if he were telling me he was a student.

"Have you had the signs?"

He shrugged his shoulders in his usual way and said, "I'm currently reading a book about Ramses II. I am fascinated by that civilization. I'd like to become an Egyptian."

I understood how very Japanese he was: he was deeply and sincerely curious about every foreign cultural phenomenon. This is why you can find Japanese who are specialists in the Breton language of the twelfth century and the motif of snuffing tobacco in Flemish art. I would have been mistaken to see a desire for identity in Rinri's successive vocations: he was interested in other people, that was all.

*

On January 9, 1991, I announced to my fiancé that I was leaving for Brussels the next day. I said it as lightly as if I were going out to buy a newspaper.

"What are you going to do in Belgium?" asked Rinri.

"See my sister and a few acquaintances."

"When will you be back?"

"I don't know. Soon."

"Would you like me to drive you to the airport?"

"That's kind of you, but I'll manage."

He insisted. On January 10, for the last time, the white Mercedes was waiting outside my house.

"What a huge heavy suitcase!" said Rinri, placing it in the trunk.

"Presents," I remarked.

I was taking all my belongings.

At Narita, I asked him to leave right away.

"I hate goodbyes in airports."

He kissed me and left. No sooner had he vanished than my throat relaxed, my heart opened and my sorrow yielded to extraordinary joy.

I laughed. I called myself every name in the book, hurled every well-deserved insult in my own direction, but nothing could stop me from laughing with relief.

I knew I should have been sad, ashamed, etc., but I couldn't do it.

At check-in, I asked for a window seat.

There is a joy greater than the joy of airports: it's the one you feel as you settle into your seat on board. This joy culminates when the plane takes off, especially if you have a window seat.

And yet my despair at the idea of leaving my favorite country was sincere, and under such conditions: it would seem that in my case the fear of marriage overrides everything. I was exultant. The plane's wings were my own.

The pilot surely flew over Mount Fuji on purpose. How beautiful it was, viewed from the sky! I composed this speech in its honor:

"Old brother, I love you. I am not betraying you by leaving. There are times when fleeing is an act of love. In order to love, I must be free. I am leaving to preserve the beauty of my feelings for you. Do not change."

Before long there was no more Japan to see from the window. But even then, the pain of separation could not annihilate my heady joy. The plane's wings were an extension of my body. What could be better than having wings? Could any name of a city ever compare with that of Las Vegas? Absurdly, that is the easiest place in the world to get married, whereas Reno is the city for divorces. To me the reverse would have seemed more justified: wings are for fleeing.

It seems it is not a terribly glorious thing to flee. That's a pity, for it is exhilarating. Flight gives the most fantastic sensation of freedom that can possibly be experienced. You sense an even greater freedom if you have nothing really to flee. A fugitive has her leg muscles in a trance and her skin all aquiver; her nostrils palpitate and her eyes open wide.

The concept of freedom has been spoken of so often that from the very first words I want to yawn. The physical experience of freedom, however, is something else all together. You should always have something to flee from, in order to cultivate this wonderful sense of possibility. Besides, you do always have something to flee—even if it is only your own self.

The good news is that you can escape from yourself. What you are fleeing in yourself is the little prison that a settled way of life will build anywhere. Just pack your bags and off you go: the ego is so astonished that it forgets to play jail-keeper. You can shake yourself off the way you'd shake off your pursuers.

Through the window, endless Siberia, all white with winter, the ideal prison by virtue of its vastness. Those who escape will die, lost in an excess of space. That is the paradox of infinite space: you sense a freedom there that in fact does not exist. It is such a vast prison that you can never leave it. Seen from the plane, this is easy to understand.

The Zarathustra inside me found herself thinking that had I been on foot I would have left footprints in the snow and consequently I could have been followed. Wings are surely a blessed invention.

So what if flight is not very honorable? It's still better than allowing yourself to be caught. The only dishonor is that of not being free.

All the passengers have been given headphones. I am going through the various musical programs, astonished that there are people on board who can actual travel to the sound of such decibels. Suddenly I come upon Liszt's Hungarian Rhapsody: my very first musical memory. I'm two and a half years old, I'm in the living room in Shukugawa, and Maman says solemnly, "That's the Hungarian Rhapsody." I listen as if it were a story.

It is a story. Evil people are pursuing good people, who are escaping on horseback. The evil people are also on horseback. So it is up to whoever can gallop the fastest. Sometimes the music tells you that the good people are safe, but that's wrong, the evil ones have devious ways of convincing the good ones that they're out of danger—all the better to catch them. The good ones see through the trick, but it's already quite late, can they escape the danger? They gallop with their lungs fit to burst, they've become one with their horse, the chase is as exhausting for them as for the horses, I'm on their side, I don't know if I'm good or evil, but I'm clearly on the side of the fugitives, my soul is that of a hunted animal, my heart is beating wildly, watch out, a precipice, can the horses make it over such an abyss, they'll have to, it's that or fall into the evil ones' clutches, I'm listening, my eyes wide with fear, the horses leap and just make it to the other side, they're safe, the evil ones don't jump, they are less courageous because they have nothing to flee, the desire to catch is not as violent as the fear of being caught, and that is why Liszt's Hungarian Rhapsody ends on a triumphal note.

I baptize the airplane Pegasus. Liszt's music has multiplied my joy a thousandfold. I am twenty-three years old and I have yet to find any of the things I've been looking for. That is why I like life. It is a good thing, at the age of twenty-three, to have not yet found your way.

On January 11, 1991, I landed at Zaventem airport. My sister Juliette was there waiting for me: I leapt into her arms. Once we had whinnied, barked, roared, brayed, trumpeted, screeched and squealed our heads off, my sister asked me, "You're not going to go away again, are you?"

"I'm staying!" I said, to put a quick end to the ambiguity of negative questions.

Juliette drove me home, to our place in Brussels. So this was

Belgium. I felt great tenderness for the low, gray sky, for how close together everything was, for the old women with their overcoats and shopping bags, for the tramcars.

"And is Rinri going to come over?" asked Juliette.

"I don't think so," I replied, evasively.

She had the tact not to pursue the matter.

Our life together picked up just where we had left off in 1989. It was good to be living with my sister. The Belgian Social Security had sanctioned our union by giving me the authentic status of housekeeper: on my documents they had written, "Housekeeper to Juliette Nothomb." You can't make something like that up. I took my vocation very seriously and did my sister's laundry.

On January 14, 1991, I began to write a novel entitled *Hygiène de l'assassin.* Every morning, Juliette left for work, saying, "So long, housekeeper!" I wrote for a long time, then I hung out the laundry that I'd forgotten in the machine. In the evening Juliette came home and favored her housekeeper with an embrace.

In Japan I had been putting a portion of my salary aside, and I had brought it home with me. I worked out that with my savings I should be able to last for two years if I lived very modestly. If at the end of these two years I had not found a publisher, I would still have time to figure something out, or so I thought, in a casual way. I enjoyed my life. The contrast with my travails in the Japanese corporation made it seem downright idyllic.

The phone rang from time to time. I was always astonished to hear Rinri's voice at the other end of the line. I never thought about him, and I could see no connection between my life in Japan and my life in Belgium: that there could be a telephone conversation between the two seemed as strange as time travel. He in turn was surprised by my stupefaction.

"What are you doing?" he asked.

"Writing."

"Come back. You can write here."

"I'm also Juliette's housekeeper. I take care of her things."

"How did she manage without you?"

"Poorly."

"Bring her with you."

"All right. You can marry both of us."

He laughed. But I wasn't joking; that would have been the one condition that might have made me agree to marry him.

The last thing he said was, "I hope you won't be taking much longer. I miss you."

Then he hung up. Never a reproach. He was kind. I had a guilty conscience, but never for very long.

Gradually the calls came further and further apart. I was spared the most sinister of all episodes, that barbarian and mendacious business known as breaking up. Except in those instances where a heinous crime has been committed, I cannot understand why people break up. To tell someone that it is over is ugly and false. It is never over. Even when you are no longer thinking about someone, how can you doubt they are still present? If someone has ever mattered, they will always matter.

Where Rinri was concerned, breaking up would have been particularly nasty on my part: "Right, you've been really rather good for me, you're the first man who's ever made me happy, I have nothing to reproach you with, I have nothing but wonderful memories, but I don't feel like being with you anymore." I would have hated myself for telling him something so hideous. It would have tainted what was a beautiful story.

I must commend Rinri for his class: he got the message without my having to tell him. Thus, it was given to me to experience a perfect affair.

One day the phone rang. It was Francis Esménard from the publishers Albin Michel. He informed me that he would publish *Hygiène de l'assassin* on September 1, 1992, in Paris. A new life was beginning.

Early in 1996, my father called me from Tokyo, "We've just received an invitation from Rinri. He's getting married."

"Well, I never!"

"He's marrying a Frenchwoman."

I smiled. Still drawn to the language of Voltaire.

In December, 1996, my Japanese publisher invited me to Tokyo for the launch of the Japanese edition of *Hygiène de l'assassin.*

On the plane from Brussels to Tokyo I felt very odd. Almost six years had passed since I had seen the beloved country I had fled. So many things had happened in the meantime. On January 10, 1991, I was a restroom attendant who had just handed in her apron. On December 9, 1996, I was an author who was on her way to answer questions from journalists. At this level you could no longer speak of social climbing: this was identity trafficking.

The pilot must have been given his instructions: we did not fly over Mount Fuji. In Tokyo there was not much that was familiar. The city had hardly changed, but it was no longer a place for me to test myself. An official car drove me to the places where journalists spoke to me with consideration and asked serious questions. I answered lightly, and was embarrassed to see how respectfully they wrote everything down. I felt like saying to them, "To be honest, it was all for a laugh!"

The Japanese publisher organized a cocktail party to launch the book. A great many people were invited. On December 13, 1996, in the crowd, I saw a face I had not seen since January 9, 1991. I ran up to him, calling his name. He said mine. I stopped short. I had left behind a young man who weighed 130 pounds; here was a young man who weighed 200. He smiled and said, "I've put on weight, haven't I?"

"What happened?"

I bit my lip, too late to call back my stupid question. He might have answered, "You went away," but he had the elegance to abstain, and merely shrugged his shoulders in his own peculiar way.

"You haven't changed," I said, with a smile.

"Nor have you."

I was twenty-nine, he was twenty-eight.

"I heard you married a Frenchwoman," I added.

He acquiesced and apologized on her behalf: she had not been able to come with him.

"She's a general's daughter," he added.

I burst out laughing at this odd detail.

"Good old Rinri!"

"Good old me."

He asked me to sign his copy of *Hygiène de l'assassin*. I have no idea what I wrote.

Other people were waiting to have their books signed. I had to say goodbye. And then a terrifying thing happened.

Rinri said to me, quite simply, "I want to give you the fraternal embrace of the samurai."

These words had an atrociously powerful effect on me. Here I was, so happy to see him again, and now I was overwhelmed by an unbearable emotion. I threw myself in his arms to hide the rising tears. He held me close, I held him.

He had found the right words. He had taken over seven years to find them, but it was not too late. When he had spoken to me of love I hadn't cared because it was not the right word. But now he had just expressed what I had experienced with him, and I had just understood. And when the right word is said, I am able, at last, to feel.

During the embrace, which lasted ten seconds, I felt everything I should have felt during all these years.

And it was terribly strong, seven years of emotion experienced in ten seconds. So that is what it was, Rinri and I: the fraternal embrace of the samurai. Infinitely more beautiful and noble than some silly love story.

Then one samurai let go of the other. Rinri had the tact to leave at once, without turning around.

I lifted my face to the sky so my eyes could to swallow their tears.

I was the samurai who had to sign a book for the next person in line.

Carmine Abate
Between Two Seas
"Abate populates this magical novel with a cast of captivating, emotionally complex characters."—*Publishers Weekly*
224 pp • $14.95 • ISBN: 978-1-933372-40-2

Muriel Barbery
The Elegance of the Hedgehog
"Among the most exhilarating and extraordinary novels in recent years."—*Elle* (Italy)
336 pp • $15.00 • ISBN: 978-1-933372-60-0

Stefano Benni
Margherita Dolce Vita
"A modern fable...hilarious social commentary."—*People*
240 pp • $14.95 • ISBN: 978-1-933372-20-4

Timeskipper
"Thanks to Benni we have a renewed appreciation of the imagination's ability to free us from our increasingly mundane surroundings."—*The New York Times*
400 pp • $16.95 • ISBN: 978-1-933372-44-0

Massimo Carlotto
The Goodbye Kiss
"A masterpiece of Italian noir."—*Globe and Mail*
160 pp • $14.95 • ISBN: 978-1-933372-05-1

Death's Dark Abyss
"A remarkable study of corruption and redemption in a world where revenge is best served ice-cold."
—*Kirkus* (starred review)
160 pp • $14.95 • ISBN: 978-1-933372-18-1

The Fugitive
"The reigning king of Mediterranean noir."
—*The Boston Phoenix*
176 pp • $14.95 • ISBN: 978-1-933372-25-9

Steve Erickson
Zeroville
"A funny, disturbing, daring and demanding novel—Erickson's best."
—*The New York Times*
352 pp • $14.95 • ISBN: 978-1-933372-39-6

Elena Ferrante
The Days of Abandonment
"The raging, torrential voice of [this] author
is something rare."—*The New York Times*
192 pp • $14.95 • ISBN: 978-1-933372-00-6

Troubling Love
"Ferrante's polished language belies the rawness of her imagery, which
conveys perversity, violence, and bodily functions in ripe detail "
—*The New Yorker*
144 pp • $14.95 • ISBN: 978-1-933372-16-7

The Lost Daughter
"A resounding success…Delicate yet daring, precise
yet evanescent: it hurts like a cut, and cures like balm."
—*La Repubblica*
144 pp • $14.95 • ISBN: 978-1-933372-42-6

Jane Gardam
Old Filth
"Gardam's novel is an anthology of such bittersweet scenes,
rendered by a novelist at the very top of her form."
—*The New York Times*
304 pp • $14.95 • ISBN: 978-1-933372-13-6

The Queen of the Tambourine
"This is a truly superb and moving novel."
—*The Boston Globe*
272 pp • $14.95 • ISBN: 978-1-933372-36-5

The People on Privilege Hill
"Artful, perfectly judged shifts of mood fill *The People on Privilege Hill*
with an abiding sense of joy."—*The Guardian*
208 pp • $15.95 • ISBN: 978-1-933372-56-3

Alicia Giménez-Bartlett
Dog Day
"Delicado and Garzón prove to be one of the more engaging sleuth teams
to debut in a long time."—*The Washington Post*
320 pp • $14.95 • ISBN: 978-1-933372-14-3
Prime Time Suspect
"A gripping police procedural."—*The Washington Post*
320 pp • $14.95 • ISBN: 978-1-933372-31-0

Death Rites
304 pp • $16.95 • ISBN: 978-1-933372-54-9

Katharina Hacker
The Have-Nots
"Hacker's prose, aided by Atkins's pristine translation, soars [as] she
admirably explores modern urban life from the unsettled haves to the
desperate have-nots."—*Publishers Weekly*
352 pp • $14.95 • ISBN: 978-1-933372-41-9

Patrick Hamilton
Hangover Square
"Hamilton is a sort of urban Thomas Hardy: always a
pleasure to read, and as social historian he is unparalleled."
—Nick Hornby
336 pp • $14.95 • ISBN: 978-1-933372-06-8

James Hamilton-Paterson
Cooking with Fernet Branca
"Irresistible!"—*The Washington Post*
288 pp • $14.95 • ISBN: 978-1-933372-01-3

Amazing Disgrace
"It's loads of fun, light and dazzling as a peacock feather."
—*New York Magazine*
352 pp • $14.95 • ISBN: 978-1-933372-19-8

Alfred Hayes
The Girl on the Via Flaminia
"Immensely readable."—*The New York Times*
160 pp • $14.95 • ISBN: 978-1-933372-24-2

Jean-Claude Izzo
Total Chaos
"Izzo's Marseilles is ravishing. Every street, cafe
and house has its own character."—*Globe and Mail*
256 pp • $14.95 • ISBN: 978-1-933372-04-4

Chourmo
"A bitter, sad and tender salute to a place equally
impossible to love or to leave."—*Kirkus* (starred review)
256 pp • $14.95 • ISBN: 978-1-933372-17-4

Solea
"[Izzo is] a talented writer who draws from the deep,
dark well of noir."—*The Washington Post*
208 pp • $14.95 • ISBN: 978-1-933372-30-3

The Lost Sailors
"Izzo digs deep into what makes men weep."
—*Time Out New York*
272 pp • $14.95 • ISBN: 978-1-933372-35-8

A Sun for the Dying
"Beautiful, like a black sun, tragic and desperate."—*Le Point*
224 pp • $15.00 • ISBN: 978-1-933372-59-4

Gail Jones
Sorry
"In deft and vivid prose...Jones's gift for conjuring place
and mood rarely falters."—*Times Literary Supplement*
240 pp • $15.95 • ISBN: 978-1-933372-55-6

Matthew F. Jones
Boot Tracks
"I haven't read something that made me empathize with
a bad guy this intensely since I read *In Cold Blood*."
—*The Philadelphia Inquirer*
208 pp • $14.95 • ISBN: 978-1-933372-11-2

Ioanna Karystiani
The Jasmine Isle
"A modern Greek tragedy about love foredoomed, family
life as battlefield, [and] the wisdom and wantonness
of the human heart."—*Kirkus*
288 pp • $14.95 • ISBN: 978-1-933372-10-5

Gene Kerrigan
The Midnight Choir
"The lethal precision of his closing punches leave
quite a lasting mark."—*Entertainment Weekly*
368 pp • $14.95 • ISBN: 978-1-933372-26-6

Little Criminals
"A great story...relentless and brilliant."—Roddy Doyle
352 pp • $16.95 • ISBN: 978-1-933372-43-3

Peter Kocan
Fresh Fields
"A stark, harrowing, yet deeply courageous work
of immense power and magnitude."—*Quadrant*
304 pp • $14.95 • ISBN: 978-1-933372-29-7

The Treatment and The Cure
"A little masterpiece, not only in the history of prison
literature, but in that of literature itself."—*The Bulletin*
256 pp • $15.95 • ISBN: 978-1-933372-45-7

Helmut Krausser
Eros
"Helmut Krausser has succeeded in writing a great
German epochal novel."—*Focus*
352 pp • $16.95 • ISBN: 978-1-933372-58-7

Carlo Lucarelli
Carte Blanche
"Lucarelli proves that the dark and sinister
are better evoked when one opts for unadulterated
grit and grime."—*The San Diego Union-Tribune*
128 pp • $14.95 • ISBN: 978-1-933372-15-0

The Damned Season
"One of the more interesting figures
in crime fiction."—*The Philadelphia Inquirer*
128 pp • $14.95 • ISBN: 978-1-933372-27-3

Via delle Oche
"Lucarelli never loses his perspective on human nature
and its frailties."—*The Guardian*
160 pp • $14.95 • ISBN: 978-1-933372-53-2

Edna Mazya
Love Burns
"Combines the suspense of a murder mystery with
the absurdity of a Woody Allen movie."—*Kirkus*
224 pp • $14.95 • ISBN: 978-1-933372-08-2

Sélim Nassib
I Loved You for Your Voice
"Nassib spins a rhapsodic narrative out of the indissoluble
connection between two creative souls inextricably
bound by their art."—*Kirkus*
272 pp • $14.95 • ISBN: 978-1-933372-07-5

The Palestinian Lover
"A delicate, passionate novel in which history and
life are inextricably entwined."—*RAI Books*
192 pp • $14.95 • ISBN: 978-1-933372-23-5

Alessandro Piperno
The Worst Intentions
"A coruscating mixture of satire, family epic, Proustian
meditation, and erotomaniacal farce."—*The New Yorker*
320 pp • $14.95 • ISBN: 978-1-933372-33-4

Benjamin Tammuz
Minotaur
"A novel about the expectations and compromises that humans create for
themselves...Very much in the manner of William Faulkner and Lawrence
Durrell."—*The New York Times*
192 pp • $14.95 • ISBN: 978-1-933372-02-0

Chad Taylor
Departure Lounge
"There's so much pleasure and bafflement to be derived from
this thriller by novelist Chad Taylor."—*The Chicago Tribune*
176 pp • $14.95 • ISBN: 978-1-933372-09-9

Roma Tearne
Mosquito
"A lovely, vividly described novel."—*The Times* (London)
352 pp • $16.95 • ISBN: 978-1-933372-57-0

Christa Wolf
One Day a Year
"This remarkable book offers insight into the mind behind
the public figure."— *The New Yorker*
640 pp • $16.95 • ISBN: 978-1-933372-22-8

Edwin M. Yoder Jr.
Lions at Lamb House
"Yoder writes with such wonderful manners, learning,
and detachment."—William F. Buckley Jr.
256 pp • $14.95 • ISBN: 978-1-933372-34-1